Anthology
2020

COVINGTON WRITER'S GROUP

COVINGTON WRITERS GROUP
ANTHOLOGY 2020

Jenny Breeden, Managing Editor
Ginny Shephard, Editing and Proofreading

ISBN: 1-945368-08-X
ISBN-13: 978-1945368-08-0

PUBLISHED BY COVINGTON WRITERS
GROUP, INC.
IN CONJUNCTION WITH
SEAGULL PRODUCTIONS LLC
COVINGTON, KY 41014

AUTHOR RIGHTS

No part of this book may be reproduced or transmitted in any form or by any means, electronic or mechanical, including photocopying, recording or by an information storage and retrieval system – except by a reviewer who may quote brief passages in a review to be printed in a magazine, newspaper, or on the web – without the expressed permission of Covington Writers Group, Inc. and Seagull Productions LLC (henceforth referred to as "the publisher").

Characters and situations mentioned and/or described in the *nonfiction* or personal narrative works contained within this book may be based on or may have been inspired by a living or deceased person or persons known to the author, unless otherwise noted by the author, and are used by the author without malice or intended harm to those persons.

Characters mentioned and/or described in the *fiction* works contained within this book are the inventions of the authors and bear no relation in any manner to any persons living or deceased with the same or similar names, unless specifically stated by the author. All incidents described herein are purely the imagination of the author, except as noted by the author.

Each author retains the copyright of their original work and has granted permission to the Publisher to include their edited work in this book.

CONTENTS

ACKNOWLEDGMENTS

The members of the Covington Writers Group would like to acknowledge all of their family and friends who have been encouraging throughout the year, keeping us motivated to continue with our writing endeavors during these stressful times. Although we have never lived through a global pandemic before and hopefully, when this one is over, we will never have to endure such hardships and devastating losses again, we now know that we are stronger than we thought we were, and we can get through this together.

On the bright side, this situation has given us so many more things we can write about—funny jokes, heart-breaking stories, and valuable insights that we can share with future generations.

Stay healthy and six feet apart, wear a mask and wash your hands.

IS IT OVER YET?

By Jenny Breeden

At the end of twenty nineteen we all joked,
"Next year we'll all have 20/20 vision."
We thought that meant everything would be perfect
That was an incorrect supposition.

Black Summer in the Land Down Under raged on.
In all, forty-six million acres had burned
And three billion animals were impacted.
Koalas were endangered, we soon learned.

Iran's response to the U.S. drone attack—
Shoot down a Ukrainian passenger jet
With one hundred seventy-six souls aboard.
"Oops, we thought it was a military threat."

The Iowa Caucus results were delayed
For more than three weeks, it was too close to call.
After all the recounts, it was still a tie.
Was this an omen for elections this fall?

The WHO declared a emergency worldwide
Which the rest of the world took seriously,
But our president said, "It's going away.
We're going to have a great victory."

Stay safe at home, wear a mask, and wash your hands
Was the expert advice we heard every day.
Non-essential businesses were all shut down.
Contactless delivery was the new way.

While in lockdown, we had new rules to follow—
Work from home, social distance, remote learning,
Visits from others via Skype, Teams and Zoom.
Getting back to 'normal' was our main yearning.

Scientists warned us that giant Japanese
Murder hornets can kill our bees overnight
But COVID-19 killed the Scripps Spelling Bee.
Really, it was cancelled. Did I spell that right?

Monkeys waylaid an Indian lab worker
Causing a panic as they made their escapes
With blood vials from coronavirus patients.
Wait, was this a plot in *Planet of the Apes*?

The Polish army invaded and held land
By crossing the Czech Republic's shared border.
"Oops, it was a misunderstanding." Really?
Why did it take two weeks to restore order?

A huge Saharan dust storm dubbed Godzilla
Crossed the Atlantic to attack the Gulf Coast.
"Dust storms are needed to nourish the ocean
And quash tropical systems," the experts boast.

They were wrong. This year was a record breaker.
Normally I wouldn't care one iota,
But, with thirty named storms in just one season,
They're using Greek names and over the quota.

Anger and outrage for Breonna and George,
Brought crowds to the streets to peacefully gather
For protest marches, some ending in riots,
With shouting "I can't breathe" and "Black Lives Matter."

If the pandemic wasn't scary enough,
You could catch bubonic plague from squirrels instead.
What's this I hear about zombie cicadas?
We're living a season of *The Walking Dead*.

Coin shortage—everyone's paying with a card.
Beauty shop closed—can't do a thing with my hair.
Home-schooling—internet access required.
Toilet paper hoarding—can you spare a square?

It's been hard coping with all these life changes.
We'll be so relieved to be able to say,
"Thank goodness, hindsight's really 20/20,"
As we celebrate our next New Year's Day.

THE YEAR I FIRED SANTA

By Mikey Chlanda

It was not one of my proudest moments.

In the town where I had my record store years ago, the Chamber of Commerce sponsored a horse-drawn carriage ride and, afterwards, a photo-op with Santa. We held it on Black Friday, trying to draw people to the local businesses rather than the malls.

A local landlord (mine at the time, as it happens) got one of his friends to play Santa. Since the landlord provided the Santa, the carriage ride started and ended at the strip mall he owned in town. This is where my record store was located at the time and more importantly, Trails Tavern.

Once each child finished his or her ride, a Chamber volunteer took the photos. So, when the child was riding around town on the carriage, Santa had some down time. While work was slow in between photo ops, Santa apparently discovered the joys of day-drinking.

With each successive ride, Santa got a little more frisky—especially with the single moms. Horrified and not sure what to do, the volunteer, knowing I was vice president of the Chamber at the time, came by my store to see if I was working.

I couldn't get hold of the president nor the director, so I had to do something. I put on my best Grinch face and marched over to the tavern.

You may be surprised to learn that it is not hard to pick out Santa in a bar. What I had not counted on was Jared, the bartender, recognizing me as I walked in. As I sat down next to Santa, Jared put a full mug of beer in front of me.

"Ah, Santa," I began, "we've had some complaints."

He hoisted his glass. "So, what the hell. It's Christmas. Cheers!" And he toasted me.

About then I wished the tavern served shots of tequila. I took a gulp of beer, swallowed hard, and prepared my speech.

"Santa, you're fired."

"Wwwwhat?" he said, slurring his words.

"Santa, I'm from the Chamber. You screwed up. You're fired. Do we owe you anything?"

"Wwwelll, Roger said he was gonna give me $50."

I counted out some twenties. "Here's sixty. Jared?"

Jared came over to us. "Yeah, Mikey."

"I need a witness that I'm giving Santa his severance pay." Jared nodded as he choked back a laugh.

I handed the defunct Santa the sixty bucks and left, throwing a five down on the bar to cover my beer.

My kid's twenty-two now. He still hasn't forgiven me for firing Santa that year.

MR. I

By Patti Kay Emerson

A few days ago, I had to go
Visit a man named Mr. I.
Nobody wants to visit this guy
If it can be avoided.
He is cruel
And makes you lie down
In a tube for nearly half an hour
While he makes a racket
Not a soul wants to hear.
He may allow you to listen to music
Through headphones in the cylinder
But you cannot hear the music
Because of his jack hammer drowning it out every few minutes
Causing you to have a headache
That you didn't have before
And when you get out of his tube,
You are in twice as much pain
As when you went into it.
In case you haven't figured it out yet,
Let me tell you.
Mr. I isn't a man at all,
But a machine.

QUARANTINE

By Patti Kay Emerson

Oh how miserable it is
Looking at four walls
All day long
For weeks on end
Always wondering
What can I do next
That is life in quarantine
Always wondering
How much longer
And being tired
From doing nothing.
That is life in quarantine.
Wanting to leave
But knowing you can't
That is life in quarantine.
Watching TV
Till you're blue in the face
Though there is nothing on
That you want to watch.
That is life in quarantine.

A VISIT

By Barbara Howard

Klara peered at the grand home on the hill. Stark against the twilight sky, the mansion gave no hint of life except for a feeble light that seeped through a first-floor window. In the distance, a low rumble warned of an incoming storm.

Closer, a gust of wind tore russet leaves from the bony-limbed trees lining the driveway. Klara shivered and pulled her sweater tight.

"Mama, I want to stay with you."

A soft voice came from the darkened car. "I promised Grandmother you'd visit. Go on Klara. She's waiting."

"But Mama . . ." She turned to find the car and her mother gone.

With leaves crunching underfoot, she scrambled up the drive, past a rickety fence, and through a rusty-hinged gate to the door. As she reached for the knocker, the door creaked open.

A woman with hair pulled into a tight bun loomed in the doorway; a mustached man hovered behind her. Klara stepped back, not liking the hot moistness that emanated from them.

"Where's Grandma?"

Gleeful grins and grasping gazes fixed on Klara. "Grandma's visiting friends. I'm Mrs. Vivant and this is my husband. She asked us to greet you. Do come in."

Klara bit her lip. She didn't want to go in. These people seemed odd with their strange eagerness and too bright smiles. "I'll wait here until Grandma comes—"

A flash of light spiked the sky, followed by a loud boom. Klara cried out and stumbled through the open door. A mantel clock chimed the seventh hour.

The dim room looked just like she remembered it. Grandma's faded sofa lolled against the wall. Limp lace curtains shrouded tall windows. The grand piano filled the center of the room with its image reflected in the ornate mirror by the staircase. She took a seat at the gate-leg table. Maybe Grandma would play checkers when she came home.

"Kla-ra," the woman's voice bubbled as if talking to a baby. "Grandma made your favorite des-sert." She disappeared into the kitchen, but the husband continued to stare, his smile too wide for his face.

She shrank back in her chair.

Mrs. Vivant bustled into the room with a slice of sugar cream pie. The scent of cinnamon and vanilla made Klara's stomach growl. She licked her lips and picked up the spoon eager to dig in. Both adults leaned forward in rapt attention.

Klara pushed the plate away. "I'm not hungry."

She moved to the sofa.

Mrs. Vivant sat next to her. "Dear, your hair is a disaster. May I brush it?"

"Disaster?"

"I mean, your hair is tousled."

"Oh." Klara touched her head.

Mrs. Vivant picked up a silver brush and pulled it through tangled gold curls. Her hot fingers stroked Klara's cheek. "So soft," she murmured, her eyes shining.

Klara scrambled to the piano bench, out of reach of brush and fingers.

"Will you play for us?" Mr. Vivant crept a little closer.

Klara ran her fingers along the keyboard. After a few random notes, she played her favorite song, *You Are My Sunshine.*

Two pairs of avid eyes followed her every move.

When the clock struck 7:30, Klara stood and started towards the stairs. "My bedtime."

Mrs. Vivant reached out her hand, her fingers twitching. "No! Don't go. Not yet."

"Stay a little longer," Mr. Vivant said. "Please. Just until Grandma comes home."

"Pretty please," Mrs. Vivant begged.

Klara studied the man and woman. Why were they acting this way? And why did they keep staring? Maybe her face was dirty. She glanced in the mirror.

The pale reflection showed a long gash circling her neck. Klara screamed and her head toppled to her hands.

And—just like that, she was gone.

"Damn it." Mr. Vivant pulled off the fake mustache. "I thought we could keep her longer this year. Joe, did you get that?"

A burly man with headphones stepped out of the kitchen. He checked the cameras and tape recorders hidden in the living room. "Sure did!"

Mrs. Vivant yanked her hair out of the bun and pulled out a microphone. "Today is October 24th. On this day, 75 years ago, 12-year-old Klara Wharton was decapitated in a car accident that also killed her mother. And just like each of the past 75 years, Klara arrived tonight at her grandmother's house at 7:00 and disappeared around 7:30 after discovering she was dead. Join *Ghosts are Real* next year. Same day. Same place. For another visit with Klara Wharton."

NO WAY

By Dana Ogden

I waited until I heard my brother Creek get up for work. He's a park ranger. When he walked outside, his sled dogs set up a joyous racket of barks and yelps and whimpers —ready to go. I wrapped a blanket around me and went out onto the porch to see if Nina was back. Nope, only five dogs were lined up.

Creek said she'd come back on her own—not to worry. She was the only Siberian Husky in the group and tended to chase whatever she saw. Today I was going to search for Nina. What else did I have to do? Creek works ten-hour days, so he won't be back until dark.

The only good thing about being shipped off to Manitoba by my mom was helping my brother take care of his six sled dogs. Guess getting suspended for being high at school was the last straw. Mom said I needed a change of scenery, time to think about my future. She said Manitoba was mysterious and magical.

What it is—is cold. It's fine, really. Besides having to spend twenty minutes getting dressed in all the layers before going outside, it's not so bad. Because my brother lives in the boondocks, I don't have to talk to anybody. No streets, no cars, no neighbors. Nowhere to buy pot or get into trouble.

After slipping on snowshoes, I took off following Nina's tracks. Luckily, it didn't snow last night, and her prints were easy to follow. She was heading north. Creek's sled dogs were named after his favorite jazz musicians—Nina, Billie, Ella, Duke, Coltrane, and Miles, the lead dog. Three were Alaskan Malamutes, two were Alaskan Huskies and one Siberian husky, Nina.

The farther I went, the fewer trees. Just snow and ice as far as you could see. It was so quiet I wished I'd brought my headphones. Mom was right about the time to think. Not much to do here besides think.

The wind started to pick up and I knew snow might erase my way home. Maybe Nina would be back home when I got there. Just when I was ready to turn back, I saw something up ahead. A small mound in the snow. I shushed forward on my snowshoes as fast as I could.

It didn't look right. She wasn't curled up to keep warm like normal. Her body lay flat on its side. Then I saw the blood. What the hell?

She'd been shot! Her body was cold. I plopped down on the snow next to her and pulled her onto my lap. Poor Nina! Was she mistaken for a coyote? Whoever shot her was a coward; they just left her here.

I had to go back soon. Creek had warned me about the cold. But I couldn't just leave her here. No way could I carry her either; she weighed almost as much as me. I pulled her closer and buried my face in her fur.

A grunt woke me. I looked up into the sad brown eyes of a polar bear.

"Are you going to eat that?" he asked.

A TERRIFIED MOTHER

By Dana Ogden

It was dangerous to be alone in the dark. Yesterday she had given birth and had fallen behind the rest of her group. Each step was draining her strength. She had to stop. As her newborn nursed, she rested. The clouds obscured any moon that might have provided light.

Tomorrow she should be able to catch up with her group at the watering hole. Kike heard something. She couldn't see far in the dark, but she could smell them. Danger! There were two. Kike had never had to defend herself alone. She moved closer to the Acacia tree putting herself between her newborn and the stalkers.

She screamed at them. Could they smell her fear? She was terrified; if she made one wrong move they'd attack.

They circled her, trying to get behind her, but she stood her ground, keeping the tree at her back. Kike called for help; maybe her group was close enough to hear. If so, she'd only have to hold them off for a while.

Growing up on the Serengeti she'd learned you never run; you face your attackers. It didn't have many predators. But two lions! Lions were good at waiting for just the right time to attack. If she could stay awake maybe help would come in the morning.

They formed a triangle, a lion at each point and her at the third. Patiently waiting, they were lying down, eyes glowing in the dark. Kike knew not to close her eyes. *Must stay awake.* Her babe was sleeping. Did she know how close they were to death's door? If these lionesses were part of a pride more lions could show up any minute.

She hoped they killed her first. She couldn't stand the thought of hearing her baby being eaten alive.

If one lion fell asleep could she kill it before the other lion had time to reach her baby?

As the horizon in the east lightened, she heard a deep rumbling. Her mom and her Aunts were coming! She saw the dust in the distance, as did the lions. They stood up and stretched.

Two lions were no match for twelve protective aunts, sisters and mother! Leading the way was Thabiti, matriarch of her herd. She charged the lions, trumpeting and swaying her formidable tusks around. The lions scampered. Everyone crowded around touching Kike and her baby to make sure they were unharmed.

Kike was exhausted. But she'd done it! Delivered her first baby on her own and protected it from harm. She had found the courage she needed to survive a night on her own. Kike was stronger now. She was a mother.

ALL I WANT FOR CHRISTMAS

By L. N. Passmore

When a phone rings near Christmas, it's either something I don't have time for or don't want to do. Or *the* person I do *not* want to talk to. Like my sister Laney. "Look," she says, "It's not like you have to give up your job and move in."

"Good. 'Cause it's a big *no* to both." I glance at the microwave timer, a minute to go. Another night of popcorn and Dr. Pepper for dinner. Looking at a stack of papers on the kitchen table, I add, "I have a ton of reports due tomorrow. Traffic's a nightmare, have to leave way early to get to the office. So, hey, Sis, can I call you back?"

Silence. I wait as Laney mentally counts to ten. Then, "Actually, no. We . . . *I* need to know. Now."

The microwave dings. Retrieving the steam-puffed bag and burning my fingers, I yelp, "You've got to be kidding."

In that despised big sister voice she declares, "It's important."

I rip open the bag and breathe in the hot essence of corn. "You do know what time of year it is, even out there in God's Country, right?"

"Right! *Exactly.*" That tone again. Then, in subtle variation, I hear, "Remember how much mom loves Christmas." Maybe the occasion softened her voice. "It would mean the world to her if you, you know, came home."

"What's the use?"

"It's not her fault, Jessie. . . I don't know how much longer our mom, well . . . you know. I can't believe Harley and McCloud would make you come in on the weekend before Christmas."

***

Christmas music. "No Place Like Home," "It's the Most Wonderful Time." Perry, Mel, Andy: the whole jolly gang belting out joy in elevators, malls, commercials, my car radio. KDKA and even WDVE have gone to a non-stop Christmas format. Inescapable. I wonder, where's the Bah Humbug song?

The going home for Christmas thing? Inevitable. Big sisters are such a pain in the ass, especially when they play the mother card. And she is right (right, right!). With the big day on a Monday, I have a long weekend. Three. Days. Back. Home. Plus a long night drive back to Pittsburgh.

As I ease onto the Interstate exit Laney's voice overrides the music. "I don't know how much longer our mom, well . . . you know. Our mom, well . . . you know." My grip on the steering wheel tightens. "Our mom . . . our mom." Nice of her to acknowledge she's my mom, too.

For a mile or so the two-lane asphalt roads, while narrow, haven't totally given in to potholes, faring better than the 'Burgh's notorious streets. At my turn by the seven mailboxes, perched on a weathered fence stand, I could go straight. Take a detour through the village, maybe stop at the shops, as advertised on the Interstate, where the locals hope for tourist dollars to cash in on Christmas. "Come home, Jessie. I don't know how much longer. . ."

Dutiful, I turn right, soon leaving behind the lined, Pennsylvania state-maintained roads. Once on West Virginia byways, I make the jump from the twenty-first century to damn near mid-twentieth. The mountains having blocked Pittsburgh's radio signals, I scan for a new station, halting when I hear "Silver Bells."

Ah, must have picked up WWVA. "Christmas time in the city. . ." Hurry-scurry, packed malls, restaurants with foreign food, and lights, Lights, LIGHTS! Not out here in the sticks. I exhale.

A slick ice coating weighs down tufts of dead grasses along the roadside. Brown fields and sagging fences show their age. Mile after mile, turn after turn, depressed cattle huddle around bales of hay tossed out to see them through the winter. Along my favorite ridge where the wind has its way with any building or tree that stands in its way, I notice brave attempts at cheer. Plastic Santas, substantial plastic, not those flimsy, dead-every-morning blow up creations. All-season reindeer, now sporting wreaths and lights, proclaim Christmas in West-by-God-Virginia!

After a commercial break, Rascal Flatts' "I'll Be Home For Christmas" snaps my attention back to the radio. I can see mom wince, shake her head, and complain "that's not Bing." I sing along, "You can count on me. . . ." Despite the noble sentiment, doubt creeps up from its hidey-hole. I glare at the speaker. It's not *my* fault Laney chose, yes *chose*, to stay with Mom. And it's not like Pittsburgh is at the other end of the country. A check of the rearview mirror fails to show any welcome distraction. I tramp the gas pedal.

The Flatts' last twanging chord gives way to Mariah's mega hit about all she wants for Christmas. Not "a lot . . . just one thing . . . just . . . you for my own." At the familiar stab to my heart (does it ever go away?), I'm thrown back to the terrible news. An accident in the mill. Nothing new in the hills—what with mines, mills, and coke plants—happens all the time. But this happened to *our* family, right about Christmas. "Damn, Mr. Dickens!"

I slow down and pull over. Look out at a wooded hillside. The slant of late afternoon sun highlights the leafless branches raised sky high. Got to admit, Mom picked up the pieces, she and Laney. But Christmas? Hard candy and oranges.

***

By the time I have my fill of Christmas nostalgia—from the angels' joyous strains o'er the plains to grandma's unfortunate run in with the reindeer—I pull into the driveway at home. Real home. The one you go back to, regardless. Because your mother is there. About to knock at the front door, I stop short. There hangs the woebegone holly wreath, once so proudly displayed when all its leaves and crimson berries gleamed.

Summoning my resolve, I sweep on in with my packages. "Merry Christmas, Sis . . . Mom . . . It's me, Jessie, home for Christmas!"

Laney calls from the kitchen, "Hi Jess, be right out," and *voila*! she appears, trailing kitchen vapors and wiping flour-covered hands on the same bargain jeans she's worn for ages.

"See you did just fine on the back roads." She's one big smile, even her voice. "Knew you'd call if you got in trouble at that turn by Kemble's Garage. This time of year no hay wagons to get stuck behind." She laughs. "Here, let me take your coat."

Laney throws my gold and black Steelers' parka at the clothes tree and wraps me in a hug. "You look great, Jessie. Really. Good to see you."

Trying not to stiffen and just relax, I get out, "You, too. *Really*. I brought wine."

For once, Laney doesn't raise an eyebrow. "Lord have mercy, red or white?"

I shrug. "Didn't know what you'd fix so brought both. Do I detect a roast?"

Laney pokes her fists into ample hips and grins. "What else? No fatted calf for the prodigal daughter, I'm afraid, but a real Yankee pot roast, fresh cut from Barger's Butchers. Do you think you can manage the mashed potatoes? Mom helped with the apple pie."

No longer able to avoid the inevitable question, I take a breath and make a stab at nonchalance. "So. How's mom doing, off to La La Land is she?"

Laney winces. "Don't talk that way. She's still our mom. Have some respect."

"Respect I got in buckets, Lane, just wish that for once . . . oh well. . ."

A wan smile floats up from the empty space in my heart. With a wave I dismiss an unvoiced thought and look into the living room. It's a comfort to see a lamp and coffee table I remember from childhood. The familiar fake Christmas tree, fully lit and hopeful, sits on a nicked piano bench, the piano long gone with a host of other family treasures. "I don't see Mom; she's here, isn't she?"

Laney pulls at the collar of her Christmas top with the angel kneeling before baby Jesus' manger. A golden aura surrounds the cherub and blessed babe. "Mom's been sleeping. Why don't you use the bathroom. I'll see if she's ready to get up."

Laney pauses and gives me the Look! The one inherited from our mother in her better days. "Don't bug her, Jess. Just go with the flow, you know?"

I watch, helpless as she battles tears. "Sure, Lane, sure. No problem. Be back in a sec."

***

Coming out of the bathroom, I see mom, a little cricket of a woman, so tiny now. She had been a beauty, Angelina Jolie hair and big brown eyes, so warm, always loving.

I sit down beside the old woman on the sofa, a three-seater. Mom had insisted, "So no one has to sit on a crack." She seems so totally complete in herself that I'm hesitant to take her blotched hand, to move too quickly. At last I pat her shoulder. "Hi mom, Merry Christmas."

She doesn't react. Just sits there. Cataract surgery had cleared her eyes. We know she can see. But today, as in so many times past, no one's home, gone to that far away country lost to time and memory. I sit beside this stranger and quietly "go with the flow." That's why I jumped when I heard, "It hasn't snowed, has it?" She smiles the old familiar smile but looks toward the window.

No, I caution myself. Don't get your hopes up, Jessie. It's just small talk. Tiny, little throw away words. *All I want for Christmas is for you to—*

Then she turns my way, tumblers falling into place, and grabs my hand.

She beams. "Jessie! You're here! Oh, my dear, Merry Christmas."

MOONSHINE AND THE ZOMBIE CATS

By L. N. Passmore

*2020 Vega Award Winner for Speculative Fiction
from the Southeastern Writers Association*

Thuds at the door jolted Sageman from his catnap. Determined to sleep, he laid his big hand on a tiny mound of growling fluffed dog in his lap and closed his eyes. "Quiet, Szechi. He'll go away."

He didn't. Then goosebump-raising wolf howls turned Szechi into a yelping frenzy.

"You got that, Kime?" Sageman's wife called from the kitchen.

"I got it Annie. Don't you mind. . . Coming, coming. Hold your horses."

He opened the door to a flood of moonlight radiating the stone stoop.

There stood a wild-eyed man about forty-five, dressed in camouflage. "What the Hell kinda doorbell's that?" he shouted. "You crazy?"

Snarling, Szechi nipped at his muddy boots.

"Don't you kick my dog, mister." Sageman snatched up Szechi to cradle him against his chest. "The doorbell is my business. You're the one disturbing the peace. Before I decide whether to turn the wolves on you or shake your hand, tell me, you and that jacket see service together?"

The rawboned, tobacco-chewing stranger slumped. "Nah, Army-Navy store." He shrugged. "Cheap. Look, don't turn your wolves on me." His suspicious eyes opened wide. "You really got wolves, Doc?" He spit a dark arc of tobacco juice.

Sageman frowned. "Not a 'Doc.'"

Standing in the blended light of the moon and the glow from Sageman's fireplace, the man leaned forward. His eyes narrowed in canny calculation. "Yeah, but you got college, ain't you? And that sounded mighty like wolves."

Sageman squared his shoulders. His face matched the stranger's hard lines.

Szechi bared tiny teeth.

"Look," the stranger continued.

"No, *you* look," Sageman cut him off. "You nearly break down my door. Say your piece and get going before I call the sheriff."

"Sorry. No need to call the law. Seen him already. Sent me to you." He looked around at the towering trees and spat again. "Your place is the devil to find."

A dense pine stand within a mass of hard woods surrounded Sageman's log home where his heart was happy. Their leaves fell like snow this late in October.

Since Sageman just stood there, tombstone silent, the stranger pressed on. "Sheriff didn't tell me 'bout no special doorbell scare the crap outta honest man. Though from what I hear, in these hills folks call you some kinda whiz—ain't nothing you can't fix. Hear you brew a mean beer and some other such to wet a man's whistle." He ran his tongue over chapped lips.

Sageman stared at the moon, thinking that he didn't need any government agents finding the tunnels. "It appears you hear too much." He looked down, scowling as he said, "Your point is?"

Keeping him waiting, his visitor squirmed. "Creepy stuff." He searched Sageman's face, now turned to stone.

"'Creepy stuff'?"

The man dug his hands into his pockets. "Sorry. It's just I'm so worried. My boy's been mauled. I'm fearful it's from them zombie cats up on the RD."

Sageman's heart thumped. Damn! *Route Demented.* He looked hard at the man's pained grey eyes. "Give me a second." He set Szechi down and tapped him on the butt. "See Annie. Go."

He turned toward the man, who had inched one boot tip over the threshold. "What's your name, stranger?"

"Ralph Teeters, from up at the trailer park above Girty's Run." He extended his hand.

After a keen gaze at Teeter's strained face and bony hand, Sageman shook it, as any neighbor would. "Call me Sageman. Come on in. You want to lose that chew, Ralph? And wipe your boots."

"Anything! If you'll just hear me out." He reached into his mouth and dragged out a lumpy plug. It disappeared into the shrubs as he scraped his boots across the stone.

Sageman led him to an easy chair on the other side of a table beside his recliner.

Landing in a heap, Teeters ventured, "Uh . . . all I'm asking is for you come and look at my boy, Lonnie, nineteen—and graduated!" He rubbed shaking hands on his Levi's. "But with his luck?" He looked down. "Lord, so low he needs a ladder to spit on a snake."

Sageman pulled out his grandfather's vintage flip-cover pocket watch with the logo of a WWII Army medic on one side, one from Vietnam soldered on the other. "Six forty-five." Pocketing the watch, he said, "Wife and I haven't eaten. . . . You?"

Teeters winced. "Feared to eat . . . don't wanna to give Lonnie ideas. Keeping a lookout so's he don't eat our cat's brains, or ourn. My old lady and me only got Lonnie's lone football helmet to share. Feared to sleep, too, full moon and all."

His gaze held Sageman spellbound. "Like I said, it happened," his voice falling to a whisper, "up on *Route Demented.* Curse that gawd-awful road! My boy can't remember now which end, both bad, middle, too."

The rigors shook him. "Must be a ghost walking my grave. Sheriff said you'd be able to help us, so here I am."

Rubbing his neck, Sageman flexed his shoulders against what felt like chafing of his well-worn shirt.

Teeters cast his sad hound dog gaze upon Sageman like he could cure leprosy. "Just take a look. And . . . could you bring . . . one of your remedies? Please?"

Sageman groaned, but true to his raising, grabbed a mackinaw and hat. Upon entering the kitchen, he pocketed a Mason jar and said, "Annie, put my food in the oven. I'm going out."

***

Sageman followed Teeters up a hill to a shabby mobile home that overlooked an iron-stained creek. Moonlight glinted off discarded bottles littering the yard.

Teeters opened a battered storm door, its window still caked with dead bugs, and stepped into the living room. "Peggy Rose," he hollered toward the hall leading to some back rooms, "it's me. I got Doc Sageman here. Come to look at Lonnie. You awright?"

"Coming," a woman answered.

"Me too, Pa," a male added. "You have the sheriff with you?"

"Not tonight, Lonnie."

Fear tinged all their voices.

Mother and son approached from the hallway. Over a white and green gingham housedress Mrs. Teeters wore a full apron, its torn ruffles splattered with spaghetti sauce, and fluffy blue slippers. Tame compared to the black and gold helmet that came down over her eyes. Lonnie wore a black T-shirt and sweat pants. He carried his bandaged left arm stiff to his side. A calico cat with tail held high followed them into the room.

Sageman set down a pint jar marked XXX and doffed his canvas hat. "Pleased to meet you, Mrs. Teeters. Your husband said you've all been having a . . . trying time." He turned to the son. "You must be Lonnie."

Dark circles accented the teen's bleary eyes. Hunching his shoulders, he nodded.

The Teeters stood mute before their guest. In the awkward silence Sageman pointed to Lonnie's arm. "While I take a look, why don't you tell me what happened. Not a doc, like my gramps and dad, but I do know something about wounds."

Coming alive, Ralph motioned them to a sofa under the window with the plastic curtains.

The unwrapping of Lonnie's left arm exposed blazing zigzag lines on puffed skin.

"You see a doctor?"

Teeters cut in quick. "And pay him with what? Empty beer bottles!"

Lonnie choked out, "I don't want . . . to eat . . . nobody's brain. Couldn't bear to hurt Bootsie." He looked over to the lounging cat. "What *am* I gonna *do*?"

Sageman offered a controlled smile. "What did you put on this, son?"

"Campho-Phenique, well that . . . and hydrogen peroxide." A sob caught in his throat. He looked to his father. "Don't want to be no zombie. I know about AIDS and all, mad cow, monkey and bird virus things. Poison leaping from animal to man. What hope do I have after getting bit by them zombie cats?"

"Always hope, son. You clean it first?"

Mrs. Teeters spoke up. "I did for sure. We're no strangers to animal bites." She shook her head, heavy with the helmet. "Don't know about zombies."

"That's just fine, ma'am. You did good work. And it doesn't work like that. First off—no cat bite turns a body into a zombie. Next, there are no zombies up on Route 57."

He stood. "Sit still there while I get a little something to help."

He picked up the Mason jar and turned to Mrs. Teeters. "I'll bother you for a clean towel, ma'am, and some gauze."

Sitting down next to Lonnie, he screwed off the lid.

Lonnie's mother handed him a thin washcloth. "All I could find."

"That will do just fine, Mrs. Teeters." He dabbed Lonnie's arm with honey-rich golden liquid that smelled like musty turpentine.

Lonnie gasped but held firm. Sageman finished, taking care to wipe up any drips. "This looks more like scratches, not bites."

He handed Lonnie the jar and said, "Take a swig. It'll do you a world of good."

Lonnie's eyes lit up. "Don't mind if I do."

"Careful there, son, that's enough. While I rewrap this, tell me what happened."

Lonnie looked to his folks.

First handing Sageman a roll of gauze, Mrs. Teeters urged, "Get on with it, son."

Lonnie took a deep breath. "Stopped at Jimmie's Bar along the river for a drink. Well, I won't lie, more'n one. Pretty late when I started up to Slippery Ridge. Moon had already crossed the hilltop over to the west where the coal chute is when I turned on to what *you* call 57. Went wrong at

that sharp bend where the three roads come together, right

before the old graveyard on the RD." He shot Sageman a knowing look. "Now you can't deny it, funny things going on up there."

His father nodded like a broken-necked chicken. "Boy's right 'bout that."

Lonnie rubbed his arm and cringed. "Seems I took couple wrong turns. Musta been two, three o'clock. Raining. First rain in weeks, dust everywhere turned sludgy. Hit a pot hole. Car shook. Felt the tire flapping and the clunk of the rim. Made a big mistake. Got out of the car."

Through clenched teeth Sageman let a slight hiss escape.

Teeters' glare spoke loud and clear: "I told you so!"

"I'm all bending down in the mud," Lonnie kept on, "looking at the tire. Busted. But I could hear them, the weeds all a rustle. At their snarls my hair nearly leaped off my head. Cripes! In the moonlight they seemed like furry alligators with long, I mean *long* tails. Their wet fur, slicky like marbled rocks. Not the worst. Had teeth like Dobermans. Cripes' sake, gleaming like they bit the moon."

"Never saw teeth like that on a cat." Lonnie shivered. "Swear their eyes were afire. They hit me while I was down. Threw my arm up. Lucky I had the tire iron. Whaled the dickens outta them. Think I heard some shots. Spitting and screaming, they took off. Left me for dead. But I made it home. Can't lie. Changed my pants."

He gave a rueful laugh. "Course the rim'll never be the same."

Looking from one distraught Teeter to another, Sageman stood. "I see you folks are in pain. No doubt about it—Lonnie's taken some scratches. Not from zombies. Cats yes, zombies no."

Ralph interrupted. "You just go and check out that godforsaken road. You'll see!"

With a warm handshake Sageman said, "Yes sir. I will."

He turned to the sad lady in the helmet. "Mrs. Teeters, now don't worry. I'm making you a promise." He cradled her trembling right hand in both of his. "If Lonnie's arm gets worse—which it should *not*—go to the Market Street clinic. Mention my name. They'll accept a flat-fee payment." He slipped her two twenties.

He put on his hat. "Lonnie, have one more swig of Sageman's Special then go to bed."

The tired heir of two GI medics went home, ate warmed up roast, and let Annie's second kiss drain away his cares.

***

Following feline yowling, Sageman drove his truck a quarter of a mile up the twisting road beyond the dump. In the wind that blew across the ridge, bare branches clattered as leaves scuttled across the road. Seeing the white-streaked sign "NO TRESPASSERS! THIS MEANS U!" he stomped the brake.

He lifted a bullhorn. "Jack-son. Jackson Burns! You hear me? Come on out here. Now. It's me. Sage. Doc's son."

In a heartbeat, two wild cats raced to the truck. He rolled up the window so only the lip of the bullhorn poked out into the chilly air.

He called again. "Jackson, you can't be far behind your little playmates. We got to talk, man." His fingers, tight on the bullhorn, ticked off a silent count to ten. The caterwauling cats spat. After cursing under his breath, Sageman made his voice smile. "Annie sent a pie and those brownies you like. . . . I brought the usual."

A shot rang out. One turkey buzzard fell from the sky. A second shot, a second bird hit the ground. On a fast burn through the weeds the cats took off.

Counting on fresh kill to keep them occupied, Sageman rolled down the window and held his breath. Sure enough, from around a pile of disintegrating boxes and dead batteries a man in tattered Vietnam era camo fatigues and a tiger stripe boonie hat appeared.

He pointed his M-16A1 rifle at Sageman. "Yo, you ridge-running moon meister. Wha' you want?"

"Like I said, man. Talk. It's been too long."

"Damn straight!" the weathered stick of a man yelled.

Sageman persisted. "How you been?"

Burns warned, "Get out" but lowered his rifle. Edging closer, he stared at the back of the truck. "What's that there for, them tiger cages? Too little for even a shucked down hoopie wreck like me."

He pointed the weapon at Sageman. "You ain't putting *my* babies in there!"

Sageman caught the verbal bullet in his teeth. "No, *you* are, Jackson. Before the sheriff and God knows who else raises a ruckus. Let's you and me talk. Please, man. Old times' sake."

After raising his rifle to ready at his left shoulder, Burns lowered it, inch by inch, never taking his gaze from Sageman. His right hand gripping the carry arm, he brought it to rest. The barrel pointed to the truck. "You say Annie sent a pie? *And* brownies?"

"Yep, and my peace offering is a quart of the good stuff."

The old war vet pulled at his grizzled beard. His hair under the boonie hat, long liberated from the post-Nam pony tail, fell in tangled shreds.

He gave a whistle then called, "Here ya, C-4*; here ya Dinky-Dau*."

Fascinated, Sageman saw two whiskered cat heads poke from a stand of wavering weeds. Through thin, black slits their gaze fixed on Burns. Almost haughty, their bodies slunk toward him, recalling Lonnie's wide-eyed description of the "zombie cats"—like furry alligators, with long tails and canine teeth.

They rubbed their arched backs and toothy muzzles against Burns' torn fatigues. He scratched behind their ears, whistled again, then gestured toward the ridge running along Route 57. "Home! Go!"

"Come on, if you're a coming," he called out to Sageman. He pointed the rifle toward his home. "You know the way."

His long legs took three strides before he disappeared into the undergrowth.

No more Burns. No more buzzards. Sageman got on with it. After all, he had been invited.

At a straight stretch the road leveled where trees came down to the storm-rutted ditches beside crumbling asphalt. Striking a whopper pothole made the steering wheel vibrate. "Slow down, Sage. No hurry to Old Madass." The guy who saved dad's life, he thought. The year all Hell broke loose. 1968, year before I was born. What, now? *Forty-six* years ago.

Once again, he could hear "Doc," as everyone called Benjamin Sageman, say: "I'd have bought the farm if it hadn't been for Corporal Burns. You're lucky you were born, son. Thank Jackson (Madass) Burns . . . and your mother, of
course."

Sageman stopped the truck. Staring through the windshield, he recalled Burns' grim face the day of Doc's funeral. The stoic vet, wearing his old fatigues, saluted when the honor guard folded the flag and gave it to Mrs. Sageman. As the bugler played Taps, he stood ramrod straight.

Sageman admired that. While the last forlorn notes faded into the bright July sky, the man who took the bullet with his dad's name on it lit a thumb-sized joint, did a smart about face, and marched away to near obscurity. Nobody said a word.

Driving on, Sageman negotiated an abrupt turn in the road at Have a Heart Animal Shelter. Relieved not to see buzzards, he smiled. Burns' cats must have gotten to the carcasses first. A half mile beyond he found the entrance to Burns' place. Dripping white letters on a weathered board spelled "TRESPASSERS WILL BE EATEN!"

In grudging admiration, he chuckled. Sign like that sure beats a wolf doorbell.

He eased down the furrowed dirt track that led to a rusting iron fence and junk.

***

Not exactly comfortable, they sat upon aluminum chairs with cracked plastic seats pulled up to a matching Formica top dinette table. The once blinding yellow tabletop and seats had turned brown. Burns' whole place smelled like a damp basement.

Arms folded across his chest, Sageman leaned back against his chair and watched his dad's old friend, a meticulous eater. His fork made surgical incisions into flaky crust and scooped up oozing bite-sized pieces of layered apples, sugar, butter, and cinnamon. Not one drop fell into a lamented splat. No crumbs defiled his scraggly beard.

Finished, Burns sighed. "Ah, Lord love a duck, just like good sex—more it satisfies, hungrier you get."

He looked up. Their gazes met.

Burns: King of Route Demented where zombie cats patrolled his high ridge kingdom, all the way from the overgrown burial ground with its lightning-blasted trees, to the charnel house of a supposed animal shelter, and then the dump.

Sageman: Protector of King Madass and his exotic cats. Doc had laid a heavy burden on his son's heart.

As if wielding a scepter, Burns pointed a broken-nailed index finger at his guest. "You've sat at my table. I've ate of your food. Seems like we're even."

Sageman held Burns's gaze. "Except for the incident the other night—your cats tangled with a kid who got lost in the rain. He's scratched bad. Family's scared to death."

"You look at him?"

Sageman nodded, hoarding his words.

"No one to blame but his damn fool self! 'Scratched.' Right? Not *bit?*"

Another nod.

"Ha! Bet you gave him a dose of your Triple Special."

Sageman cocked his head, noncommittal.

"No proof C-4 or Dinky-Dau had anything to do with your pissant 'incident.'" Burns slipped a Mark II combat knife off his belt and placed it on the table. "So you and this kid and his folks got diddly squat."

Leaning forward, Sageman placed his spread-fingered hands flat on the table. "*Except* he gave a spitting image description of cats— never found natural in *these* hills. You old Papa-san, you've got to protect your 'babies.'"

"Protect *them!*" Burns's fist thumped his chest. "They protect *me*. You don't wanna know what crawls out of that graveyard up the road." He bolted up, knocking over his chair that clanged on the cement floor. Blood drained from his gaunt face, turning it skeletal.

Being cautious, Sageman stood, but hesitated to touch his host. "Jackson? Hey man!"

Burns threw his arms around something invisible. Then his body convulsed. "Sweet Jesus, I'm zapped!"

Almost caught off guard, Sageman leaped to catch him. *God! After all these years . . . Nam'd to Hell.* He willed himself to remain calm. "Jackson," he said, one decibel above a whisper. "You remember Doc, your friend. I got you, Madass. I got you, man. Me, Doc. You saved my life. Took my bullet. I got you now. No worry. Hang on."

Lost between worlds, Burns choked out, "Don't let them . . . turn me into . . no body bag ghost."

"No way, Corporal Burns." Sageman propped Burns against the table.

Burns breathed heavily. "If I do . . . buy the farm . . . swear the cats keep guard."

"Sure. Sure," Sageman said. "Look, I've got some A-number-one GI hooch. He unscrewed the lid of the Mason jar and held it up to the man lost in a firestorm forty-six years old. "Here, Corporal, open up."

As ordered, Burns took a gulp, swallowed fast, and took another swig. Shaking his head like a wet dog, he barked, "Hot Damn!"

Sageman held him in his arms.

***

After maneuvering Burns into a chair at the table, Sageman sat beside him for an hour. It felt like a year. Through labored breaths the haunted man stared into Sageman's eyes. He blinked and tried to clear his head. *"Doc?"*

Sageman recognized the look, the same one his dad had carried until the day he died. His son had badgered him
to talk about the war.

Finally, Doc cut all questions short. "Tet Offensives. First assault—eighty thousand VC* and NVAs* crawled out of their tunnels. Poured over the DMZ. Attacked everything in sight. We beat them back but, my God, we took casualties. No matter the color of the skin or the slant of the eyes, son. All blood is red."

Burns wiped his mouth on his sleeve. "No, no," he said. "You're *not* Doc?" His eyes widened. "I know you. Doc's *son!*" He patted Sageman's arm. "I swear, you look just like him."

He poked Sageman's breast with his finger. "Bullet ain't no thing, son. Doc took care of me. Brothers in war, ya know." His expression turned thoughtful, eyes sad. "Seems like we're all walking dead. 'Cept your dad. Left the World* behind."

Though he shook his head, Burns smiled. "Doc helped me get my cats out of the mountains, used the tunnels. Gift from the *Montagnards*. French name, but we just called them 'Yards.' They got it 'bout ghosts. Cats eat them."

Sageman nodded, smiling back. "There it is. Now we've got to take care of your cats so they can deal with the ghosts."

Burns grabbed the younger man's shoulders. "You ain't gonna to take them away!"

"No, man. No way." Sageman laid his left hand along Burns's haggard face, the other on his shoulder, as much to brace as comfort him. "But you have to secure them until we're sure the boy's OK. No rabies. Keep them here, but locked up. Care for them—outside, inside, whatever, man. That'll be enough to keep the ghosts away until C-4 and Dinky-dau can go back on patrol.

Won't be like the tiger cages back in Nam. I promise."

Burns's whole body shook. He rocketed back and forth from Vietnam's Central Highlands to Route Demented. Sageman held on.

***

Back, body and soul in West, by God, Virginia, Burns grabbed the table before looking around the room. "You say something about brownies?"

Sageman laughed, grateful—if not totally sure they were out of the woods. Not waiting, he pulled back a cloth from the wicker basket he had brought. The aroma of chocolate, really sweet chocolate, flooded the air.

Blowing a silent whistle, Burns broke into a smile. "How about you and me wash down these *special* brownies with the rest of your Triple X and then go get them cages. I guess C-4 and Dinky could do with some R and R at their own personal Holiday Inns."

Sageman hoisted the Mason jar. "Down the hatch."

*GLOSSARY

Ain't no thing:	No big deal
C-4:	Plastic explosive
Dinky-Dau:	Crazy
DMZ:	Demilitarized Zone
NVA:	National Vietnamese Army
VC:	Viet Cong
World:	USA

ALL THE UNHAPPY MEN

By Gary Reed

Chapter 1
Monday, Noon

It was the gun that caught Penny Lieber's attention.

She had just stepped from The Enquirer building, hoping to find somewhere quick and cheap to get lunch. But the first thing she noticed wasn't the hot dog stand at the curb or the Korean couple who ran it. And it wasn't the muscular black man with a red bandana wrapped around his head, standing in front of the cart, or his annoying habit of sniffing repeatedly. The first thing that grabbed Penny's attention was the semi-automatic handgun he was pointing at the Korean couple.

The hot dog stand vendors were busy gathering money from their cash box and apron pockets, shouting angrily at the man as they did.

"I call police on you," Mrs. Lee yelled.

Mr. Lee said, "You all alike."

The man with the gun shouted back, "Why don't you go back to wherever you came from?"

Cringing at the racial taunts but edging closer, Penny pulled her smartphone from her pocket, turned the camera on, and pointed it at the scene.

She remembered a photojournalist saying that lay people never get close enough to what they're trying to capture. When they think they're close enough, he told her, they should move halfway between that spot and what they want to photograph. She stepped closer and positioned herself to get a better angle.

The Korean couple reluctantly handed over their money.

The robber grabbed the cash with his free hand and stuffed it into his pocket.

Mrs. Lee shouted, "You mother a filthy whore."

Ready with his wittiest retort, the man with the gun said, "Did you kill your neighbor's dog to make those hot dogs?" He sniffed and turned to make his escape.

Penny hadn't meant to be in the man's way, but she was. "I'm a reporter for The Enquirer," she blurted out. "Can I get your name for my story?" It was her first day in her first job after college, and it felt good to be able to say, "I'm a reporter."

DeShay Smith, the man with the gun, wasn't about to tell a reporter his name. He muttered an obscenity and tried to step around her.

Penny was a petite five foot three inches, although in her pumps she stood a little taller. "It's my first story as a reporter," she pleaded.

The man gave her a shove and hurried off down the sidewalk, sniffing and grumbling about white-chick stupidity. He shoved the pistol into his waistband, but in the excitement, he forgot to take his finger off the trigger.

The sound of the gunshot surprised Smith. Then the pain registered.

The sound of the shot startled Penny as well. She flinched and ducked reflexively. Unblinking, her cell phone camera panned the sky, the cars in the street, and finally the sidewalk.

Recovering quickly, Penny focused her camera on the man. She videoed him struggle three steps and collapse, muttering an obscenity. Blood stained his crotch and ran down his leg.

Penny moved closer.

The man was on his back on the sidewalk, struggling to pull his pants down, evidently wanting to assess for himself the damage to his manhood. He punctuated the effort with obscenities.

Someone, Penny thought, would have to edit out those obscenities before The Enquirer could put this video on its website. And then it occurred to her that's not what she should be worrying about. She should be using her phone to call 9-1-1. But before Penny could complete the call, a police cruiser, lights flashing and siren on, pulled to the curb. With its lights flashing and siren on as well, a second police cruiser drew to an abrupt stop behind it.

The officers exited their vehicles, drew their guns, and approached the suspect warily.

The first police officer, a heavyset black woman, used her foot to nudge the hotdog-stand bandit's gun away from where it lay on the sidewalk. The second officer secured the weapon. The policewoman told the bloodied, panicked man that an ambulance was on the way and demanded his name.

DeShay Smith whimpered, "I shot my dick."

"Is that your first name or last?" the second officer asked. He was a white male, about forty.

The female police officer ignored her colleague and demanded again that the man on the sidewalk, holding himself to stop the bleeding, give her his name.

He said, "DeShay Smith."

Penny found her notebook and jotted down the name.

"Mr. Smith," the policewoman said, "I'm placing you under arrest. You have the right to remain silent—"

The Korean woman from the hot dog stand pushed her way through the circle of onlookers and told the policewoman, "He got my money. Make him give back."

In a loud voice, the policewoman said, "Everybody, step back. Give us some room. To the Korean woman, she said, "We'll get your statement in a minute."

Penny glanced around at the people who had gathered to gawk.

"You too," the policewoman said to Penny.

"I'm a reporter," Penny said. "Officer, can I get your name?"

"Get back," the policewoman insisted.

Is that your first or last name? Penny wanted to say but didn't.

In the minutes that followed, the police officers restrained DeShay Smith, an ambulance arrived and carted him off. Bystanders made cruel gibes about how it served him right. Penny obtained statements from several witnesses, and when there was nothing more to be done at the scene, she hurried to the newsroom.

Penny had spent the morning in Human Resources filling out paperwork and listening to a series of lectures about the company's anti-discrimination and HR policies. Penny had watched most of that on video recordings—as if their content wasn't dull enough. None explained what to do or not to do if a man robs a hot dog stand and ends up shooting himself in the wiener.

When Penny located the newsroom, her first order of business was to find her new boss, someone named Nick Costello, whom she was supposed to see at one o'clock. It was ten till. Someone told her Costello was in a meeting. Someone else said he went to lunch.

Penny had graduated just two weeks earlier from Ohio State University with a journalism degree. She was determined to prove that she had what it took to do the job despite her age and inexperience. She persuaded Dan Walsh, a veteran reporter, to let her use his computer to write her story about the holdup and self-inflicted gunshot injury.

Thirty minutes later, when Costello returned to the newsroom, Penny introduced herself and handed him her first story. For a twenty-two-year-old who had always wanted to be a reporter, it was a proud moment. "I've got video too," she said.

"I'm sorry," Costello said. "I knew you were supposed to start today but forgot. What's your name again?"

Chapter 2
Tuesday Morning

On Tuesday morning, Penny was scrambling to get herself together and out the door when her phone rang. It was an assignment editor with news of a shooting in Cincinnati's West End. *Could she cover it?*

Penny gulped and said, "Sure."

The assignment editor gave her an address.

Penny said, "On my way."

Before she rushed out the door, she stopped and ran through a mental checklist. Purse? *Yes.* Keys? *Yes.* Cell phone? *Yes.* Notebook and pen? *Yes,* and *yes.*

She stepped through the door into the hallway and realized she hadn't put her shoes on. It took her only a moment to locate the right shoe. Three minutes-plus to find the left.

Mental checklist again.

Out the door.

At the West End address the assignment editor gave her, the only sign of a shooting was the police car at the other end of the block, disappearing around the corner. If there had been an ambulance, it too had left. Penny considered trying to follow the police car but thought better of it. She parked and knocked on the door of the ground floor apartment matching the address the assignment editor had given her.

A tall, angry black woman answered.

Penny introduced herself and said, "My assignment editor said there was a shooting here."

"That was my dumbass boyfriend."

Penny found her notebook and pen. "What happened?"

"I already told the police."

"I'm new," Penny said, "and I'm a woman. The police won't tell me anything." She had no idea if that was true but thought it might appeal to the fierce woman standing in the doorway.

The woman rolled her eyes.

Penny gave the woman a plaintive smile. "The guys at the office will laugh their butts off if the new girl shows up without a story."

The fierce woman said, "You're gonna make me late for work."

"If somebody shot your boyfriend," Penny said, "I think they'll understand."

The woman stepped back and said, "Well, come in, but hurry up."

Penny followed the woman into the apartment and sat where she pointed.

The woman said, "I ain't got no coffee. This ain't Starbucks."

"That's fine," Penny said, her voice more irritable than she intended. "Can you tell me what happened?"

"Ain't nothing to tell. My dumbass boyfriend went out to his car and plopped down in the driver's seat, 'cept like an idiot, he forgot he'd left his gun on the seat. Must have gone off, 'cause next thing I know, he comes rushing back in here and runs into the bathroom. He was dripping blood, so I went to see what he'd done. He pulls his pants down, and his thing's all messed up."

"He shot himself in the penis?" Penny asked. As she did, she realized, to her annoyance, why the assignment editor had wanted her to cover the story.

"Dumbass nearly shot it off!"

Penny grimaced.

"He was trying to wipe the blood off it. I told him he couldn't fix it here. He needed to go to the hospital."

"What's your boyfriend's name?"

"Ex-boyfriend. If he's that stupid, I don't want nothing to do with him. Know what I'm saying?"

"If he shot his manhood off," Penny paraphrased, "you don't want anything more to do with him?"

"You got that right, sister, but you can't put that on TV."

"I work for the newspaper, The Enquirer."

"Whatever."

Penny took a breath and tried again. "What's his name?"

"Len Perry."

"Do you know where the ambulance took him?"

"Don't know, don't care."

"How old is Mr. Perry?"

"Thirty-eight."

"Do you know why he left the gun in the car?"

"Because he ain't supposed to have no gun, and he knew if he brought it in here, I would have told him to get his ass out."

"Why isn't he supposed to have a gun?"

"He's got a record, honey." The woman shook her head and muttered something Penny could not make out.

"Does Mr. Perry have his own place?" Penny asked. "I'm looking for an address."

"He *was* living here, but when he gets out of the hospital, I'm sending him packing."

"One last question, then I'm out of your hair. What's your name?"

"I don't want my name in no newspaper."

Penny nodded. "You're my source. I need your name for my notes."

"Jasmine Jenks."

"Thank you, Ms. Jenks. Can I have your phone number too, in case I forgot to ask something?"

To Penny's surprise, the woman rattled off a phone number.

Penny asked, "Is that your cell?"

"Yeah, but now I got to get to work."

"I'm leaving," Penny said, standing. "Where do you work?"

"Cincinnati Bell."

Penny thanked the woman and left.

Penny didn't own a gun, and neither did anyone she knew. But when she got to her car, without giving it a thought, she glanced at the seat before she sat down.

At the newsroom, Penny learned how to determine which police officers responded to the call and how to reach them. She also learned how to find out where the ambulance took Len Perry and how to contact the hospital's information desk to determine his status.

Then, she hurried off to University Hospital, hoping to get a statement from DeShay Smith, the previous day's penis shooter.

Mr. Smith didn't want to talk to her.

"Well, can you tell me," Penny asked, "were they able to save your penis?"

"My lawyer," Smith said, "says not to talk to anyone about what happened."

"He doesn't want you talking about robbing that Korean couple. I'm sure he didn't mean that you couldn't talk about what happened in the operating room."

"I don't want to talk about that either."

"Can I ask where you got the gun?"

"You can ask, but I ain't gonna answer."

"Did you buy it from a gun store?"

Smith thought a moment and said, "No, I didn't get it from no gun store or Walmart or anything like that."

"Did you get it from a pawn shop?"

Smith shook his head. "Nah. Nothing like that. I bought it from someone."

"So, no background check?"

"No. I just paid cash."

"Was this your first arrest?"

"Oh, hell, no."

"Do you have any felony convictions?" If he had, Penny knew, he wouldn't be allowed to own a gun and wouldn't have been able to pass a background check.

"Just a couple," Smith said, "but I don't think I'm supposed to talk about that."

"I can look up your record," Penny said. "Telling me won't change anything." She hadn't learned how to look up someone's record and wondered if, in fact, a reporter *could* look up someone's criminal record. And if she'd be able to look up guys who asked her out.

"I ain't never dated a white girl," Smith said. "Do you think you and me could go out when I get out of here?"

"I can't date people I write about," Penny said. Actually, HR hadn't said anything about that. Still, she was pretty sure it was a rule, and in any event, it sounded more professional than what she wanted to say.

"If it's any consolation," Penny said, "another guy shot himself in his crotch this morning. He's still in surgery. Maybe later, you two can talk and compare notes."

"That's cold," DeShay Smith said. "That's cold."

Chapter 3
Tuesday Afternoon

When Penny made it back to the newsroom, she had a pleasant surprise. There sat a bouquet of roses on her desk.

Josh Wilson, the guy she had dated for the last two years, had sent them. "Congratulations on your new job & for making the front page on the first day. Way to go!"

Penny thought the gesture and note were sweet.

Two weeks earlier, just before graduation, Josh had proposed, and Penny had reluctantly turned him down. They were both about to graduate. They were also both about to start their first "real" jobs. And she had just signed a lease on her first apartment of her own. "Let's give ourselves a chance to adjust to all these changes first," she had said.

Her refusal had evidently surprised Josh as much as his proposal had surprised her—and had hurt his feelings.

Josh said that if she had commitment issues, then maybe they should start seeing other people. After all, he was going home to Cleveland, and she was going home to Cincinnati.

After that, Penny feared she would never see Josh again.

She smelled the flowers. Evidently, Josh was having second thoughts and wanted to rekindle their relationship.

For the first time that day, Penny smiled.

Chapter 4
Early Wednesday Morning

A little after five Wednesday morning, Penny's cellphone, recharging on her nightstand, jangled. An assignment editor wanted her to cover a shooting at the Greyhound Bus station.

Penny was sure she was having a nightmare.

"I can't have you fall back to sleep," the assignment editor said. "Get out of bed and tell me you're standing up."

Penny buried her head under the pillow and counted to ten.

"Okay," she told the man on the phone. "I'm up."

The editor warned her, "You're going to have to get there quick, or everybody will be gone."

Reluctantly, Penny dragged herself out of bed, got dressed, and hurried downtown.

At the Greyhound bus station, she learned from Sam Ackerman, the bus driver, that the incident occurred on a bus traveling from Atlanta to Chicago. Just before 5:00 a.m., the bus made its usual Cincinnati stop at the Gilbert Avenue station, near the casino. That's when the shooting occurred.

"The only reason I'm still here," Ackerman told Penny, "me and the passengers, is because we're waiting for the company to deliver a new bus." He shook his head.

"What happened?" Penny asked.

"The floor on that bus has some blood on it," he explained, pointing to the bus, "and someone at headquarters is worried about infection."

"How did the blood get there?" Penny asked. "Did someone get shot?"

"It's just a few drops of blood," Ackerman complained. "I don't know why they don't just have someone clean it up and be done with it."

Penny despaired of finding out from the driver what had happened and turned to the passengers.

The bus riders were more helpful. The bus had just pulled into the station, they told Penny, when they heard a single gunshot. Almost immediately, a man jumped up and ran to the restroom at the back of the bus. No one knew the man's name, but most agreed he was white, short, thin, and had long hair. He apparently had a loaded handgun in his pocket, and it had gone off.

Penny circled back to Sam Ackerman, the bus driver. Penny filled him in on the account she had put together.

"Sounds about right," Ackerman said, "but I could be wrong."

"Did you get the man's name?" Penny asked.

"The cops did," Ackerman said.

"You don't have his name?" Penny asked.

Ackerman mulled over her question and said, "I imagine the paramedics got it too."

After Penny left the Greyhound Bus station, she looked for a Starbucks. When she found the nearest one, Penny learned something she would not have discovered if she had tried to cover the shooting later in the day. In Cincinnati, even Starbucks wasn't open at five-thirty in the morning. She had to go to White Castle for coffee.

She was barely three days into the job, she fumed to herself. And already, she'd gone from wearing a nice suit and drinking coffee from Starbucks to wearing Dockers and buying coffee from the drive-through window at White Castle.

It was too early, she decided, and she was in no condition to start calling people. She went home, slept for an hour, took a shower, and started her day over. Her new rule was: *If it happens before Starbucks opens, it wasn't her story.*

On her way into the newsroom, she swung by the Cincinnati Police Department and chatted up police communications specialist Delmar Payne. He identified the man on the bus as Stanley Larkin, a 21-year-old Atlanta man, on his way to Chicago. The shot nicked his penis and creased his upper thigh. One of the officers found the handgun in the toilet.

Penny asked if the officers had charged the man.

"It's still under investigation," Payne said. "But he had twelve more handguns in his overnight bag. We're trying to figure out if he was planning on selling them—or just, you know, feeling really insecure."

"Does this sort of thing happen all the time?" Penny asked. "I just started Monday, and this is my third story about some guy shooting himself in his crotch."

"No, no, no," Payne assured her, laughing. "I've been here twenty years, and I've never heard of so many guys shooting themselves in their privates in one stretch like this. Our accidental shootings usually involve someone leaving a loaded gun where a kid can get ahold of it. Those stories are pretty sad all the way around." Payne shook his head. "Especially when a toddler finds his parent's gun and kills himself or his sister or another toddler."

Later, in the newsroom, Penny found her boss and demanded to know if assigning all of these shootings to her was some sort of initiation ritual. "Is that why you're making me cover all of these guys shooting themselves in their privates?" Her voice sounded, at least to herself, a bit too high strung and shaky.

Costello, her boss, chuckled. "No, this isn't an initiation ritual. I'm hoping you can figure out what's going and do some sort of wrap-up article." He suggested she should find out if this string of incidents was related to recent legislation allowing gun owners to carry concealed guns without a permit. "Talk with some experts and maybe some gun owners and see what you can put together."

Penny knew that made sense but still suspected it was just a rationalization for assigning all of these incidents to the "new girl."

Costello said, "Penny, you're doing a great job. I've never seen someone get on the front page their first day here—let alone stay there."

Mollified, Penny did an online search, looking for local firearm instructors. She also found a local gun rights blog called GunCinnati.com.

She made a list of firearm instructors and started calling.

Chapter 5
Wednesday Midday

The University of Cincinnati produces many of the city's doctors, lawyers, and other professionals, as well as a large share of its college graduates. With an eclectic mixture of traditional older buildings and frenetic modern structures, its sprawling campus dominates Cincinnati's Clifton neighborhood—and makes parking there hard to find.

Just after eleven, an assignment editor sent Penny to Clifton to cover yet another shooting. He gave her no information other than an address on McMillan Street, near the university.

When she arrived, paramedics were attending to a man who was screaming and crying incoherently. Nearby, two police officers were interviewing witnesses. A tow truck operator, summoned to remove the injured man's illegally parked car, arrived just after Penny. He double-parked next to her little Toyota.

Penny sized up the situation and realized that if she didn't move quickly, the paramedics would whisk the victim away before she could get a statement from him. She approached the poor guy, who was still shouting incoherently. Hoping to calm him, she took his hand.

That seemed to quiet him momentarily.

"My name is Penny Lieber," she said. "I'm a reporter with The Enquirer. Would it be okay if I rode with you to the hospital?"

"We can't allow that," the lead paramedic snapped. "I need you to step back."

The paramedic's name tag identified him, unpronounceably, as "Smrcka." Penny assumed that was a misspelling. She ignored the paramedic and patted the injured man's hand reassuringly. "Sir, are you married?" she asked. "Can I notify someone for you?"

The man was dark-skinned, bearded, and wore a turban. He shouted something long and incomprehensible in what Penny assumed was a foreign language.

The paramedic insisted, "Ma'am, let go of his hand. We've got to get him in the wagon."

The man on the stretcher grunted in pain and babbled something unintelligible.

Penny looked at the paramedic and said, "He wants me to go with him."

Smrcka, the paramedic, gave her a disbelieving look.

"Are you married?" Penny asked him.

"No," the paramedic said, a quizzical look on his face. "Please move aside."

Penny gave him her best smile. "Can I get your phone number?"

The paramedic smirked. "Sure. It's 9-1-1."

"I'm serious," Penny said. "Would you go out with me?"

The paramedic studied Penny for a moment. "If you want to go with him that bad, get in. But just so you know, he doesn't speak English."

"He doesn't?"

"I don't think so."

"Oh." Penny thought a moment, glanced again at the injured man's turban, thick beard, and uncomprehending expression. She turned back to the paramedic and asked, "Can I get your phone number anyway?" She had no intention of asking him out but thought it would help build up her list of contacts.

Smrcka, misspelled or not, rattled off a number. "Do you have a card?" he asked.

"Not yet. I'm new. What happened to him?"

"He shot himself in the penis. The bullet went through a testicle too. Sorry, but we've got to get him to the ER."

Penny stood aside, and the paramedics lifted the stretcher into the ambulance.

As they did, the injured man screamed.

Penny winced and reluctantly turned and headed toward the policemen. They were wrapping up questioning two guys she assumed were students. But as she approached, the policemen turned and started toward their cruisers.

Penny shouted, "Officers!"

The cops, both white males in their thirties, stopped and turned.

"I'm a reporter with The Enquirer," she said, hurrying toward them. "Can you tell me what happened?"

The taller—and older—of the two police officers spoke. "We're still trying to figure that out, but those two—" he nodded in the direction of the students, "—say he pulled to the curb and began to exit his vehicle, when there was a loud noise, and—"

The second officer interrupted. "He shot himself in his junk, getting out of his car."

Speaking in a firmer, more formal voice, the first officer retook control of the narrative. "When Mr. Abdullah exited his vehicle, the witnesses heard what sounded like a gunshot. Mr. Abdullah let out a scream, and—"

Penny interrupted. "Mr. Abdullah? That's the guy they just put in the ambulance, right?"

"Yes, ma'am. At least that's what his driver's license says."

"You were saying?" Penny made a mental note of the officer's name. "Hudepohl." Like the beer.

"After what sounded like a gunshot, Mr. Abdullah took a step or two and then fell to the sidewalk, screaming in pain."

Nice detail, Penny thought.

"Apparently, Mr. Abdullah had a pistol in his waistband, and when he exited the vehicle, it discharged. The bullet struck him in—"

The cop hesitated.

The second cop, the slightly younger and better looking of the two, finished the thought. "The raghead shot himself in his dick."

The first cop shot his partner a look. "The bullet went through Mr. Abdullah's penis and testicle."

"Did you get his full name?" Penny asked.

"Abdullah Abdullah," the first cop, Officer Hudepohl, said. "He's probably from Afghanistan."

Penny tried to think about what else she needed to ask. "Are you going to charge him?"

"With what?" Officer Hudepohl asked.

"I don't know," Penny admitted. "Discharging his weapon? Criminal stupidity?"

Officer Hudepohl said, "Is there anything else you need?"

"Can I get your full name?" Penny asked.

"Chad Hudepohl."

"Did you serve in Afghanistan?"

"Two tours. Is that it?"

Penny thanked him.

Officer Hudepohl turned and headed toward his vehicle.

The second cop introduced himself as Andy McKee. He gave Penny a Cincinnati Police Department business card with his name and cellphone number on it. "In case you have any more questions."

"Thank you," Penny said, grateful.

"By the way," McKee said, "If you're looking for a date, you should call me. I'm way better looking than that paramedic."

She noticed that McKee did not have a wedding ring.

Chapter 6
Wednesday, Late Afternoon

Penny brought up Google on her computer and formulated a search. She wanted to know if there was a connection between states allowing anyone to carry a concealed weapon without a permit and men shooting themselves in their privates. Penny identified several states that had recently changed their laws to allow concealed carry without a license. She also found more stories of men carrying guns in their waistbands and shooting themselves. But no one—so far, at least—had made a connection between that and guys shooting themselves in their junk.

"Junk science," Penny muttered to herself, "hasn't caught up with this."

Google *did* turn up something called the Gun Archive, which listed both fatal and nonfatal shootings, based mainly on media reports. The site had picked up the mishaps she had covered earlier in the week and included links to her articles. Penny sat up a little straighter in her chair.

Maybe someday a researcher would search the archive for incidents of guy-shoots-self-in-his-privates, she thought. And perhaps they would figure out if those incidents happened more often in states that changed their laws so any idiot can carry a concealed gun without a license. But if anyone had already done that research, her Google search hadn't found it.

Google also didn't tell her what to say when her mother called and complained.

"I don't know why you only want to write stories about men who shoot themselves down there," her mother said. "I would think you'd want to write about something else."

"Mom, I *do* want to write about something else," Penny said, "but I have to cover the stories the editors tell me to cover."

"After all that education," Mrs. Lieber said, "and all you write about is this?"

"Mom," Penny said, hoping to change the subject, "Josh sent me flowers and a nice note."

"I don't know why you let him get away."

Penny had already explained to her mother, several times, why she hadn't been ready to marry Josh. "I think maybe he wants to rekindle things," she said, hoping to end the call on a positive note.

"Penny, that train's left the station. When a guy decides he's ready to get married, he'll marry the first woman who'll have him."

Penny rolled her eyes.

"Mark my words," her mother insisted. "Before you know it, he'll marry some other girl."

After the call from her mother, Penny tried to refocus on her wrap-up article. She checked the local gun rights blog, GunCinnati.com. She was surprised to see that she was the focus of the blog's wrath.

The blog noted that The Cincinnati Enquirer had published several stories that week reporting on incidents in which men had "allegedly" shot themselves in their crotches. The blog continued:

> *Don't get me wrong. Anyone who carries a gun in his pocket or sticks it in his waistband is not a responsible gun owner. I'll go further than that. Anybody who does that is an idiot. But the Enquirer claims that several of these incidents have happened in Cincinnati this week. That's as many as usually occur in the whole country in a year. There's just no way that many guys shot themselves in their junk in Cincinnati in less than one week.*
>
> *This is an obvious attempt by the lamestream media to make gun owners look like a bunch of irresponsible idiots. It's part of the massive conspiracy to cram gun control and ultimately gun confiscation down our throats!*

The blog entry ended with a big reveal:

> *If that sounds unhinged, consider this. All of these stories have the same byline, "Penny Lieber." I checked, and that*

byline only appears on these stories about guys shooting themselves in their privates. That byline didn't exist before this week, and it doesn't appear on any other article. Obviously, the Enquirer made up that byline because none of its reporters wants to put his name on news stories that are FAKE NEWS.

Penny hit the comment button and typed:

I'm Penny Lieber, and I'd like to interview you for a story I'm doing. Please call the newsroom and ask for me. If I'm not around, leave a message. I need to know if you can come to the Enquirer newsroom for an interview and what would be a good time for you.

PS: You might want to call the Cincinnati Police Department media relations office and ask if the incidents in my reporting are real.

Chapter 7
Thursday Morning

On Thursday morning, the GunCinnati.com blog reported that someone had contacted him, pretending to be the reporter "Penny Lieber." "Like I'm stupid enough," the blogger wrote, "to fall for that!"

Penny was still stewing over the blog post when Delmar Payne, the Cincinnati Police Department's media relations specialist, contacted her. He had a tip on another shooting.

"A doofus was posing naked for a selfie when he accidentally shot himself in his privates," Payne explained. "I thought you would want to know."

"Hey, thanks," Penny said. "Give me his name, and if he asks me out, I'll be sure to tell him no."

Payne laughed. "Christian Baxter, age 25. Lives in Carthage."

"When did this happen?"

"Last night, about ten."

"Really, thanks," Penny said. But she worried that now even the police department considered her beat to be men who shot themselves in their private parts.

Penny found Baxter in Good Samaritan Hospital, where the hospital listed him as in satisfactory condition. He was talkative and funny and not bad looking, but he struck Penny as more than a little self-absorbed.

"I was taking a selfie," Baxter told her. "I wanted it to stand out from the rest of the shirtless-guy-with-a-gun selfies, so I decided to go Full Monty."

Penny took notes as fast as she could.

Baxter grimaced and adjusted how he laid in the hospital bed. The usual assortment of tubes connected his body to the usual array of IV bottles, monitors, and other hospital whatnot that Penny preferred not to think about.

"I was trying to thrust my hips around," Baxter said, "but the gun went off instead of the camera."

Penny tried not to let her face show what she was thinking. She asked the first thing that occurred to her. "Did the police charge you?"

Baxter grimaced again. "Yeah, but I think they're going to drop the charges."

"Why?"

"The cops who arrested me made a bunch of jokes about being glad someone as stupid as me won't be able to reproduce. My attorney is threatening to sue the city for mental distress, and he thinks they're going to drop the charges in exchange for my not suing."

"What does your girlfriend think?" Penny asked, guessing Baxter intended to send the selfie to a girlfriend.

"She dumped me," Baxter said. "She said if I intended to send the photo to her, she didn't want anything more to do with me, and if I intended to send it to some other girl, I could go to hell." He chuckled to himself.

"Are you going to be okay?" Penny asked. "I mean, physically."

"The doctor thinks so, but I'm pretty uncomfortable now."

"So, you're not out of the gene pool after all?"

"Nah. But my shooter is out of action for a while."

Chapter 8
Thursday Afternoon - Evening

On Thursday morning, Jevonte Moore bought a gun from a stranger in Louisville, Kentucky, in a deal he arranged through Armslist.com. He bought the gun for cash in a Dairy Queen parking lot in Louisville's South End.

By Thursday afternoon, he was back in Cincinnati on his way to sell the gun to someone in the parking lot of a convenience store in Cincinnati's Northside neighborhood.

Near the store, Moore decided to pull into a parking lot and check to make sure the gun worked. When he removed the weapon from its case, he accidentally squeezed the trigger and shot himself in the genitals.

Moore had a prior felony conviction, making it a crime for him to have a gun. Cincinnati Police officers Chad Hudepohl and Andy McKee arrested Moore. They were the same District 5 police officers Penny met the day before in Clifton, where the Afghan man had shot himself.

Andy McKee tipped Penny off to the arrest, and she agreed to meet him for drinks after work. They met at a bar in Clifton that was a cop hangout. Penny bought beers on her expense account—a first for her. Not wanting to end up with a DUI on her record, she nursed the same beer all evening.

Andy introduced her to several other officers. Chad Hudepohl, who had a wife and kid at home, wasn't part of the group.

In response to her questions, Andy explained the difference between "concealed carry" and "open carry." He also said that gun zealots contend they have a Second Amendment right to a carry concealed gun without a license. They referred to that as "constitutional carry."

One of Andy's cop friends volunteered another term. He called the practice of carrying a pistol in a waistband "castration carry."

The evening wasn't all about educating the newbie on guns. In addition to the cops, Penny met Liz Nadler, a local ATF or Alcohol, Tobacco and Firearms agent. Liz was a few years older than Penny but was also the only other woman in the group. She and Penny struck up an immediate friendship. During a trip to the ladies' room, Liz told Penny that Andy McKee was definitely into her.

Penny learned that Andy had an Associate Degree in Criminal Justice and a nice sense of humor. Plus, he looked good in a uniform. She imagined he would also look good without one.

Chapter 9
Friday Morning

"A local man shot himself in the penis with a pink pistol Thursday evening, prompting the Cincinnati Police Department to urge safer gun handling," Penny typed. She figured that would suffice for the lead, and if it didn't, the copy editor could fix it. She had decided she officially hated covering these stories.

"According to police," Penny typed, "Tony Tanaka, 27, was handling his girlfriend's handgun while they were on the way to the grocery. When they arrived, Tanaka stuffed the gun into his waistband. That's when the gun discharged.

"Tanaka, who works at the Toshiba plant in Northern Kentucky," Penny added, "declined to comment."

Penny's cell rang. It was her mother. Penny sighed and took the call.

"Penny, it's your mother."

"Hi, Mom," Penny said. She had tired of explaining caller identification and the unique ringtone she had assigned to her mother.

"Penny, dear, your father and I are worried about you."

Penny doubted her father had much to do with whatever it was that was bothering her mother.

"We don't understand why you only want to write about these men shooting themselves."

"Mom, I told you. I'm the new person. I don't get to decide what stories to cover. I have to cover the stories the assignment editors tell me to cover."

"Couldn't you tell them you want to cover something more, well, more uplifting?"

"You think I should tell the assignment editors I want to write about sports bras?"

"You know what I mean."

Penny bit her tongue.

"Anyway, even that would be better," Mrs. Lieber said, "than writing about these men shooting themselves you-know-where."

"Yes, Mom, I know where."

"Don't get snippy."

"Look, I'm sure this string of idiots shooting themselves will end soon." Penny hit the enter key on her keyboard to make sure her computer didn't lock. "This has just been—"

"My friends," Mrs. Lieber said, "must think you hate men."

"Mom, I dated Josh for two years. Just because we broke up doesn't mean I've given up on men." Penny closed her eyes in frustration.

"Are you seeing someone else?" Mrs. Lieber asked. "When's the last time you went on a date?"

Someone placed two message slips on her desk. Penny glanced at the first one. It said her boss, Nick Costello, wanted to see her.

"Last night," Penny responded to her mother, "but I can't talk about it now. My editor wants to see me."

"Is he married?"

"Who?"

"Your editor?"

"Mom, I've got to go."

"Tick tock. That's all I'm saying."

"Bye, Mom."

The second message said, "The selfie guy called. He wants your phone number."

Chapter 10
Friday Afternoon

Penny's evening of beers with cops and her chance acquaintance with Liz Nadler, the ATF agent, paid off Friday afternoon. Liz gave Penny a heads up on a developing   situation.

"You didn't hear this from me," Liz said, "but a guy was heading up Reading Road when he decided that another driver, a Hispanic dude, cut him off. After some horn honking and hand gestures back-and-forth, this guy decides to take a couple potshots at the Hispanic dude. Trying to get away, the Hispanic dude drives up onto the sidewalk. The white guy is trying to keep up and shoot at the same time. He ends up crashing into a utility pole."

Penny removed her glasses and rubbed her eyes. Then it dawned on her. Liz hadn't said anything about the guy shooting himself in the crotch.

"He didn't shoot himself?" Penny asked, to be certain.

"No," Liz said. "Anyway, the white guy's got a shitload of guns and ammunition in his car. And a bunch of Neo-Nazi crap."

"What's his name?"

"Let's see, I got that here. Ephraim Johnson, 57, Saylor Park. He's so fat his nickname is 'Round.'"

Penny jotted that down and said, "Got it. Thanks. How many guns is a shitload?"

After checking her notes, Liz said, "Seventeen, all told, most of them AR-15-style semi-automatics. But here's why I called. My office is working on getting a search warrant for his home." She read a street address. "If you leave now, by the time you get there, they should be ready to go in."

Penny thanked Liz again, let the assignment editor know where she was going, and hurried off to the address Liz gave her.

When she arrived, ATF agents, FBI agents, and Cincinnati Police officers were traipsing in and out of the house with what they found inside. The final tally was thirty-four more guns, over a hundred large-capacity ammo magazines, three kilograms of marijuana, and nine kilograms of methamphetamine. They also removed boxes of Neo-Nazi and white supremacist stuff.

When Penny wrote up her scoop, she put the shooting and seizures in the context of recent mass shootings by white supremacists. That guaranteed her story would land on the front page. It also meant that other news outlets would repackage her article and run it.

After she turned the story in, she gave Liz a call to thank her again. "That's my first story that didn't involve a guy shooting himself. I owe you," she said. "Big time."

"Here's how you can repay me," Liz said. "My boyfriend wants to have a three-way."

Penny hesitated. "Ah, I'm not into that."

Liz let out a big laugh. "Only kidding! Look, I gotta go."

Liz's tip wasn't the biggest surprise of the day. That surprise came late afternoon in an email from Josh Wilson, her ex.

"Penny, I wanted you to hear this from me," Josh emailed. "I've gotten engaged. She's a great gal. I hope you'll be happy for me."

Penny was determined to show some class and not react angrily. Her first response was, "Congratulations, Josh." She bit her lip and then typed, "This sounds kind of sudden. How long have you known her?"

"I met Macy last semester," Josh said, "but we only got serious a month, six weeks ago."

That meant they first "got serious" *before* he asked her to marry him.

Get a gun, Penny imagined replying. *And stick it in your waistband.*

What she actually wrote was, "Josh, good luck—and thanks for letting me know."

Chapter 11
Saturday

Penny had Saturday off, which meant she had a day to do laundry, clean her apartment, do her grocery shopping, and pay bills. And run to Walmart to get a birthday present for her bratty nephew. She put Walmart and grocery shopping off until after lunch and gathered up her laundry.

A couple hours later, after pretending a bowl of Ramen noodles was lunch, she rushed through her shower, got dressed, and made sure she had the note with the name of the toy her nephew wanted. She headed out to Walmart.

On the way, the radio reported a mass shooting in Texas late the evening before. Several lawmakers offered thoughts and prayers, but Penny was sure that gun legislation wasn't in their thoughts and didn't have a prayer in Congress. She changed to another station. It ran a clip of Cincinnati's Congressman, Stefan Schwanz, saying it was too soon to talk about preventing the next mass shooting.

At Walmart, Penny found a parking spot that was less than a marathon run from the store. She told herself it must be her lucky day. The usual short, thin, vaguely disreputable-looking men stood outside the store, smoking cigarettes. The men stood apart from one another and cast furtive glances at arriving shoppers as if expecting their disapproval.

Inside the store, Penny looked in vain for a Walmart employee who could help her find the toy she wanted. The effort disabused her of the notion that today was her lucky day.

Penny was about to give up when she heard what sounded like the sound of a dropped pallet hitting the floor. Or maybe gunfire.

From unseen speakers in the ceiling, a disembodied voice boomed, "Attention Walmart Security. Code Brown. Code Brown."

Penny guessed "Code Brown" was a veiled reference to a shooter—or maybe to the color of the Walmart security guard's underwear about then.

She looked around. She saw a jerk who appeared to maybe 18 or 19 come out of the sporting-goods-and-guns section of the store. Like the smokers outside the store, the man was short and thin. But unlike them, he was dressed in black, wore tactical gear, and held an assault rifle.

The gunman looked at Penny with cold, remorseless eyes.

Penny felt her body go cold.

The man raised the gun.

Penny shouted, "I'm a reporter!" She tried to move.

The man fired.

Later, when the police were securing the crime scene and counting the dead, Officer Chad Hudepohl stopped before a body he thought he recognized. He called to fellow 5th District police officer Andy McKee, who was nearby.

"Andy," Hudepohl said, "isn't that one the girl from the newspaper?"

Chapter 12
Saturday Afternoon

"The shooting today at Walmart," Cincinnati's Congressman Stefan Schwanz told reporters, "is sad, and the victims will be in my thoughts and prayers. But I'm not going to politicize this tragedy. It's too soon to be talking about how to prevent the next shooting. And I'm certainly not going to demonize the many responsible gun owners in this country because of the irresponsible actions of one individual."

Dan Walsh, a reporter from The Enquirer, asked, "Can you arrange for there to be no more mass shootings until it *is* the right time to talk about preventing them?"

Representative Schwanz shook his head in disgust and said, "Next question."

"Congressman," the Enquirer reporter shot back, "is that what you would say to Penny Lieber's parents? She's in your thoughts and prayers, but you're too in bed with the NRA to do anything constructive?"

"I understand Ms. Lieber was a colleague of yours, and you're upset," Schwanz said, "but that question is totally out of bounds." Schwanz rubbed his nose vigorously.

"Is it true, Congressman," a reporter from an alternative news rag asked, "that you're sleeping with an NRA lobbyist?"

"That's a complete fabrication. Fake news!"

"Is that why your wife is divorcing you?" another reporter asked.

"Absolutely not," the Congressman said, his face an angry red. "We're done here." He turned abruptly and walked away.

Later, a 19-year-old, sitting in his room in his parents' home with an unloaded AR-15 rifle in his lap, watched the exchange on television and smirked. He pointed his gun at the image of the Congressman's back and pulled the trigger.

Note:

News reports of self-inflicted injuries from guns carried in waistbands and pockets, none of which occurred in Cincinnati, served as the inspiration for this story, but this is a work of fiction.

Names, characters, businesses, places, events, locales, and incidents are either the products of the author's imagination or used in a fictitious manner. Any resemblance to actual persons, living or dead, or actual events is purely coincidental.

YIPPEE

By Alvena Stanfield

The old woman loaded a small bottle of water into her purse and began her half-mile walk to the grocery. A few blocks from home she saw a child around eight years old, holding onto a fence badly in need of paint.

"Did you see a little black dog?" the child sobbed.

"What? You're asking me?" The old woman looked around as if someone else was nearby.

"Yes, his name is Yippee." The girl paralleled her hands, showing he was about eight inches tall. "He's black and this big."

"Did he get out of the yard today?" the old woman said.

The child nodded, tears making tracks down her face.

"If I see him, I will bring him back to you," the old woman said and continued toward the grocery.

The clerk allowed the old woman to put a note on the bulletin board in the store's window. "Lost. Small black dog" and added her phone number. Standing in front of the pet food, she counted the coins in her change purse.

"Bologna four dollars, bread two."

She slipped the cheapest can of dog food into her purse.

"Five eighty-three," the clerk at the checkout said.

She handed the clerk a five-dollar bill and two quarters, two dimes, four nickels and ten pennies.

"Six dollars," the old woman said.

The clerk shrugged and returned her seventeen cents. But at the door, an alarm sounded. The bagger grabbed her elbow and took her to the manager. He leaned close to the manager and whispered something. Without looking up, the manager nodded.

"I think you forgot to pay for something, Ma'am," the manager said and smiled. He studied the frail, withered woman wearing a faded housecoat and a straw hat, a sunflower tucked into its band.

"Oh, please don't call the police. I had to. You see. I had to. Please," she said.

Had to what?" the manager said. He stepped around the counter and stood alongside her, his hand on her shoulder.

Lowering her head, she drew the can out of her purse and held it toward him.

"Seven hundred a month doesn't go as far today as it used to," she said.

"But dog food, Ma'am? You're broke, living on bologna sandwiches and feeding a dog?"

"No. I'd love to have one. I had my dog Shadow for nigh onto eleven…"

"So why did you steal dog food? Surely you don't eat that stuff, do you?" the manager tilted his head, listening.

"It's, it's not for me. A little girl lost her dog. She said his name is Yippee. If I see him, I want him to follow me. I only have enough bologna to last me for…" The old woman shook her head.

The manager studied the ceiling and its flickering neon light.

"If you're short on money, why are you doing this? Is this child your niece or . . .?

The old woman shook her head. The manager bit his lip, studied the old woman's skeletal hands and shook his head.

"Come into my office," he said.

"Oh no. You're calling the police? It won't happen again. I've never done this before," the old woman sobbed.

Shoppers nearby stared at them. The old woman leaned away from him. He gently pulled her into his office, moved a chair close to his desk and picked up his phone. The old woman let out a cry and held her fist against her mouth. He patted her arm.

"I'm calling the shelter. Maybe they picked up a stray."

"Tell them he is small and black, maybe a pup. His name is Yippee and belongs to a poor little girl," the old woman said. She wrung her hands while she listened to the manager talk to the shelter. He shrugged.

"No, they picked up a black cat but no pups," he said and reached into his pocket. "Look, I can't allow stealing, so go pay for it."

"Oh, bless you, sir, thank you," the old woman said, squeezing the dollar tight in her hand.

"And don't tell anyone this happened, is that a promise?" he said.

The old woman nodded, hurried to the checkout and left before the clerk could give her change.

***

"Yippee, Yippee, come here, Yippee," the child was still sobbing at the fence.

"I got a nice can of dog food for him if I see him," the old woman said. The child nodded and shrugged her shoulders.

"I wish I could help," the old woman said, as she studied the child's huge elbows and knees jutting from limbs thin as sticks. "Would you like a sandwich?"

The child gazed at the bag the old woman carried and opened the gate. The old woman followed her to the porch at the back of the house. Picking her way among beer cans and cigarette butts, the child sat on a swing hanging from rusty chains.

"Will it hold both of us?" the old woman said, studying the swing's rusty clamps and hooks.

The child licked her lips. The old woman eased herself onto the swing. It creaked as it moved the least bit. Ignoring the danger, the old woman emptied the bag onto the area between them.

"This is how I like to eat my sandwich," the old woman said and folded a slice of bread over a slice of bologna and took a bite. The child frowned and looked toward the yard.

"Would you like to try one?"

The child nodded and reached for the old woman's sandwich.

"Let me make you one, maybe two?"

The child nodded. In a New York second she polished off the first sandwich and reached for the second.

"I'll keep my eye out for Yippee," the old woman said as she gathered up the half loaf and half empty bologna package.

The back door flew open. A woman dressed in a nightgown, holding a cigarette stepped out barefoot onto the porch.

"What'cha think yer doin' there with my kid?" the woman said.

The child bolted into the yard toward the front.

"She asked me to look for her pup. We had sand…"

"Dog? She don't need no damn dog. Get out of here," the woman leaned toward her. The old woman grabbed the bag, bread and bologna and hurried off the porch.

At the gate, she gave the child a quick hug.

"I'll try to locate Yippee. I promise," she said. The child nodded and, leaning against the fence, watched her as she walked toward home.

***

For a couple days, the old woman received no response from the note she'd left at the grocery story. She traveled several blocks searching. Each day she ended her search in front of the little girl's house.

"Didn't see him. But any day now, somebody will read my note and call," she said and daily handed the child a folded bologna sandwich.

***

The phone rang.

"Are you looking for a little black dog?" the caller asked.

"Why yes, he's a little girl's pet. Do you have him?" the old woman's face flushed as she smiled.

"No. But I breed cocker spaniels. AKC registered. I have a ten-week-old and one of my girls just had another litter four weeks ago. So, I'll let him go cheap, say, a hundred."

"Dollars?" the old woman said.

"What else? I sold his litter mates for four."

The old woman leaned against the wall and shook her head.

"Are you still there?" the caller said.

"I wish I could locate a hundred dollars. That little girl really misses her Yippee."

"Well, try the pound," the caller said and hung up.

A week later, the phone rang.

"You still looking for a black pup?" she said.

"Why, yes. I take a walk every day, but..." the old woman said.

"Well, I'll let him go for twenty-five. I've got six-week-olds ready to go. But you get no papers for him."

"Oh, that's wonderful. But I don't have a car. Can you bring him to me?"

The caller sighed and hung up. Next day the breeder called and told her she changed her mind. She'd bring the pup around 3.

The old woman hurried to the bank and filled out a withdrawal slip for $25.

"Sorry, Mrs. Wilton, your checking's down to $15."

The old woman's dropped shoulders and lowered chin revealed her disappointment.

"Seven hundred doesn't go as far as it used to. You remember my son Jason used to add money. But he got laid off so all I have is my pension."

The clerk took a deep breath. "Tell you what, I'll loan you $25 and you can pay me back two dollars each check," the clerk said, reaching for her purse.

"Oh, thank you. That's a deal," the old woman said and hurried home.

She phoned the breeder who dropped off the plump, wiggly, black cocker spaniel pup. He whimpered. The old woman sat in her rocking chair and petted the little dog until both napped. When they woke, she went to the door but found night had fallen.

"Too late for an old lady to go falling on some sidewalk," she told the pup. She gathered up a few towels and placed them alongside her bed. The pup stood on the towels looking up at her, his stub of a tail vibrating left and right.

"Oh, you are adorable, Yippee" the old woman said as she turned off her light. The pup whimpered, then yipped, then let out whopping sad wails.

"Hush, the people in the apartment upstairs will hear you," she said as she turned on the light.

The pup stood alongside the towels looking up at her, tail wagging.

"I see you're going to win, aren't you?" the old woman said as she picked him up and laid him alongside her. The pup stayed quiet overnight and chewed a hole in her quilt.

***

"Yippee!" the little girl said, reaching toward him, as the old woman approached the fence. She handed the pup and the half-empty can of dog food to the child.

"Now, he cannot take care of himself. You alone have to make sure he has food and water, you understand?"

The child nodded and squeezed him against her chest.

"And don't let him out of the yard," the old woman said. As she headed back home, passersby stared at her tears but did not ask questions.

***

Throughout the rest of the summer and fall, the old woman strolled past the little girl's house in late afternoon. Often she would see them playing there. Sharing her bologna sandwiches became a ritual between the three of them. She paid the two dollars each check to the bank clerk with a smile and a thank you.

As the first snow melted, the old woman headed to the grocery store. She stopped at the child's fence. Horrified, she saw half-grown Yippee lying in muddy, partially melted snow, tied to an abandoned bicycle wheel, the rope tight around his neck, Frozen water in a bent pie pan lay nearby, his dirty food dish empty.

Her feet slid on the unshoveled walkway as she picked her way to the back door. She knocked, waited, knocked several more times. A man with grease-embedded hands, wearing a mechanic's overalls, opened the door. The smell of stale cigarettes and beer wafted out.

"I was just wondering if maybe the dog out there," she motioned toward the bicycle wheel, "might need a doghouse, and maybe a blanket, Sir," the old woman said.

"Nope, He's no business of yours. Damn useless thing just showed up here one day." He pushed the door half closed.

"Oh, your little girl said her dog ran away, said his name was Yippee," she said.

"That damn lying kid. Yeah, she calls him Yippee. Never had a dog till somebody dropped that one off."

"Oh, so you didn't, you don't want him?" she said.

"Hell no. He barks half the night till I beat him a little, tracks mud all through the house when she sneaks him in." He raised his eyebrows. "You want to buy him?" he said.

The old woman looked down at her feet. "How much?" she said.

"Thirty bucks. He's a cocker, you know," he said and coughed. "Worth every penny."

"Yes, I believe you. I'll come back tomorrow," she said.
She phoned her son.
"Jason, can you give me thirty dollars?" the old woman asked.
The pause at the other end of the phone answered her.
"Till my next check comes?" she said.

BUZZED

By B.B. Wellstone

Sherry lurks in the aisle of feminine hygiene products. The other players probably won't find her here, and that's what she wants. The game is stupid. She doesn't want to play anymore.

They're playing Frog Mart Tag, named in honor of the establishment in which it takes place. Frogwood, Texas, pop. 8,947, isn't large enough to attract a chain store, so an enterprising Frogwood family—the Carsons—developed Frog Mart in a former cattle barn. The Frog Mart logo is a maniacally-grinning cartoon frog face which Sherry finds ridiculous. Yet the logo and the store both seem to be successful: Mrs. Carson, matriarch of the Carson Clan, drives a bright green Mercedes with vanity plates advising everyone to B FROGGY.

Josh, the unofficial leader of the group, invented the game. Similar to normal tag, you play inside Frog Mart, as the name suggests. And obviously, you can't do much running. That would attract too much attention. The trick is to act like you're shopping while trying to tag one of the others—if you're It—or keep from getting tagged if you're not.

Sherry wonders why she's even playing. Well, she's not, really; she's just pretending to play. But why is she even doing that? If there were an award for the dumbest, most pointless game in the universe, then by God, Frog Mart Tag would win. She can think of about ten million other things she'd rather be doing on a Saturday afternoon.

They're all going to get in trouble. Some dude's been watching them, following them around. Aw, jeez—there he is, just a few feet away. Pretending to look at tampons. Seriously? He might as well have the words "SECURITY GUARD" tattooed onto his forehead. In a minute, he'll probably say, "Please come with me, Miss." Then he'll call Sherry's parents, or maybe even the cops, and she'll be dead. Her dad, a former Army sergeant, will yell at her for hours and ground her forever.

The other players, she knows, won't get into much trouble at all. Josh's dad died years ago. His mom works two jobs and seems constantly on the verge of either falling asleep or having a nervous breakdown. She'll be too tired and frazzled to care what Josh has been up to. Plus, like everyone else, she seems to think Joshy-Poo is perfect.

Christi's mom, a school psychologist, will try to analyze why Christi gave into peer pressure. Then she'll take Christi on a therapy shopping trip.

The Taylor twins, Tom and Aaron, are destined to become politicians, attorneys, or televangelists. With the perfect mix of embarrassment and astonishment, they'll charm and lie their way out of trouble. Their story will be that they didn't know what was going on, that they just happened to be here while the others made bad choices.

Jill, the token Angry Emo of the group, for sure won't face any parental wrath. Her mom and dad will be too busy screaming at each other to care what's going on in their daughter's life.

Sherry picks up a box of pads, pretends to study it, then tosses it into a shopping basket. (She grabbed one earlier, to hide the fact that she has no intention of buying anything.) She watches the security guard dude out of the corner of her eye. After a moment, he walks away.

She breathes a sigh of relief and places the box of pads back on the shelf.

She's beginning to wish she'd never joined this group. But what else was she supposed to do? They moved back to her parents' old hometown after her dad retired from the Army. Her other schools were near military bases where kids moved in and out all the time; being The New Kid was no big deal, and there was a culture of instant acceptance.

Not so here. New Kids are about as rare as space aliens, and they're treated like such. Worse, even. They're treated like space aliens who also happen to be infected with COVID, herpes, and Elephant Man's Disease. She spent the first month of school eating lunch by herself, feeling like the biggest loser on Earth.

When Jill asked her to sit with her group, Sherry thought she'd died and gone to heaven. Normally, she'd have been put off by Jill's appearance. The girl was straight from Central Casting, playing the part of the rage-filled, misfit beauty: tall and wispy-thin, wearing black jeans, black Doc Martins, and quarter inch-thick black eyeliner. Sherry might well have refused Jill's invitation back at her old school. But here at Frogwood High, at this point, Sherry would have jumped at the chance to sit with Charles Manson's group.

She's been sitting at Jill's table ever since. Hanging out with her and the rest of them on the weekends. Doing all kinds of fun stuff. Stuff like . . . Frog Mart Tag.

Yay.

"Hey." The whisper comes from inches behind her. Speak of the devil: it's Evil Genius Josh, the Charlie Manson of the group. His mask is covering the lower part of his face, but she can still see that he's smiling at her in that We've-Got-Ourselves-A-Secret way that's guaranteed to make hearts flutter. In all honesty, that smile sent Sherry's heart fluttering a time or two . . . before she knew him well enough to become immune.

"What's up?" She keeps her tone as casual as possible while thinking: Please, please, PLEASE let this stupid game be over.

"Let's go see him," Josh tells her. "He's here. The Whistler."

Sherry doesn't respond. Is this a new twist on Frog Mart Tag that he's just made up? Hopefully, it doesn't involve shoplifting. Or killing anyone.

"You've heard of The Whistler, right?" Josh is still smiling.

"Um, no."

"What!" Josh reacts as if she's never heard of Lady Gaga. "No way! The Whistler is Frogwood's local crazy guy. He tries to talk to birds. By whistling."

Sherry wonders if this is true. Josh might have seen this guy whistling to himself, the way guys will do sometimes, and decided to concoct the story for no good reason other than to mess with people. Because that's how he rolls.

"Is he outside?" Sherry thinks if they leave the store, Josh might decide to end the game.

"Yeah, he's outside. Talking to his fine feathered friends. Come on, you can see him in action."

Sherry follows, noting that Josh's nicely-muscled rear is clad in yet another new pair of designer jeans. (Christi is possibly the only other teenager in Frogwood with as many outfits.) Sherry has no interest in making fun of a crazy guy, if that's what The Whistler really is. But maybe Josh doesn't plan on actually making fun of him. He probably realizes that irritating a crazy person could be hazardous to your health, and he'll just point the guy out to her. It'll be no big deal.

The others are waiting at the end of the aisle. Josh already rounded everyone up, it seems.

Tom, the cattier of the Taylor twins, snickers.

"Couldn't you decide which brand of feminine hygiene product to go with?"

Jill rolls her eyes. She makes a motion as if to flick her hair back in exasperation, then seems to recall that she now has a crew cut—a teal crew cut with purple highlights, as a matter of fact. "Can it, Taylor. Sherry's a girl, all right? The secret's out."

"Whatever." Tom starts to say something, probably a smart-aleck remark, then shuts his mouth. Good move, Sherry thinks. Jill's not only the Emo Queen of Frogwood High; she's also the Queen of Sarcasm, and Tom's totally outclassed.

They all remove their masks as they walk out of the store and toward one of the little islands in the parking lot. Each island has a patch of weedy grass and a scorched-looking sapling. One of them also contains a man in his mid to late 40s. Sherry assumes the man standing in this parking lot island is The Whistler.

He doesn't look the least bit crazy to her. Not that she's an expert on what crazy people look like.

Josh nudges her.

"What did I tell you? Watch."

The man is staring into the branches of the sapling, seemingly oblivious to the gang of teenagers fast approaching. As they come closer, Sherry notes that the guy's attention is focused not on the sapling itself, but on a bird perched on one of its branches.

The man starts whistling at it.

Josh and the Taylor twins guffaw, and Christi giggles.

"Okay, Sherry sees him." Jill sounds bored. "And you're thrilled, right? Let's go hang out at my house. My parents aren't home from their counseling session yet. We can watch YouTube and get out of this freaking heat."

Jill veers away from the others, but Sherry hesitates.

"Come on. Let's go," Jill urges. "They're just gonna be jerks."

Sherry follows. She looks back and sees that the others are, indeed, being jerks. Josh and the Taylors are whistling, flapping their arms, and circling the guy. Christi, watching on the sidelines, is doubled over in laughter.

Sherry feels like she ought to do something, but she's not sure what.

"Why don't they just leave him alone?" she asks.

Jill shrugs. "They should. The poor guy's been through enough."

"Yeah? Like what?"

Jill sighs. "It's a really sucky story. The guy's son was a few years older than me, so I didn't know him that well. He was in my brother's class. Not a bad guy at all, from what Brock told me. The guy was huge—I mean, muscly huge, not fat huge—and he also had a crazy-bad temper. Finally ended up getting expelled his senior year."

Sherry thinks: Muscly huge + crazy-bad temper = recipe for disaster.

"What'd he do to get expelled?"

"He walked into the restroom one day and saw a couple of guys bullying some geeky Freshman. Really sick stuff, as in practically molesting the kid. And he went off. Busted the one bully's nose; gave the other one a concussion."

"They expelled him for that? They should've given him a medal."

Jill nods, then regards the group of kids still tormenting the man. She sighs, then turns away from the spectacle.

"A lot of people thought the same thing. But, I mean, he did hurt those guys pretty bad. Almost ended up in Juvie. So, after he got expelled, he joined the Marines. Did a couple of tours in Afghanistan. And did pretty well . . . until he got killed by a sniper."

She glances over her shoulder at the others, confirms that they haven't tired of their "Let's Harass the Town Crazy Dude" game, and shakes her head. "So, anyway," Jill continues, "Dad, there, apparently believes that his son's been reincarnated. As a bird. So when he whistles at birds, he's actually trying to communicate with his son."

"Are you freaking kidding me? No! Freaking! Way!"

Sherry spins around and marches to the island with no clear idea of what she's going to do. She reaches Josh first and grabs one of his arms in mid-flap.

"Cut it out!" she yells. "All of you! Like, right now!"

The others regard her as though she's just farted loudly during a funeral. The Whistler looks at her calmly, then turns his attention back to the branches of the sapling.

The bird flies away.

Josh shrugs, walks toward Jill. The other kids follow—except for Sherry.

"Sir," she says hesitantly to the man. "I . . . I just wanna apologize. For my friends' behavior. It's . . . really inexcusable. And, also . . . I'm sorry for your loss." She swallows, feeling like she should say more. Realizing that her mask is still dangling from one ear loop, and that she's standing closer than six feet from the guy, she hurriedly puts it back on. "Like, I'm SUPER sorry for your loss," she adds lamely.

The Whistler turns toward her. His expression hasn't changed; he still appears calm, almost serene.

Then Sherry sees a tear snaking down his cheek.

"Um, okay. Good-bye, then," she concludes awkwardly, shrugging and walking away.

Sherry reflects that she's accomplished quite a bit this afternoon. For one thing, she's spent several hours at a game that even the stupidest individuals on the planet might consider a total waste of time. Even better, she's now returned to her previous status of friendless loser. She turns away from the group and heads toward her own neighborhood.

But then Jill yells, "Hey, Sher. My house is this way," as if Sherry doesn't know, and motions for her follow. The sun reflects against Jill's multi-colored hair, transforming the space above her head into an unlikely, garish blue halo.

Relief floods throughout Sherry's entire body, and she fairly skips toward Jill and the others. The Whistler is no longer on her radar at all.

Now they're in Jill's basement, watching YouTube. There's been no mention of what happened in the Frog Mart parking lot. Apparently, The Whistler's no longer on anyone else's radar, either.

Josh lets out a yelp, startling everyone.

"Dude! What's your problem?" Aaron, the normally quiet half of the Taylor Twins duo, scolds.

Josh is waving both hands around his head.

"It's this psycho fly," he explains. "Keeps buzzing around me. I can't get rid of it."

"You know what flies are attracted to," Jill says in a bored monotone befitting her persona of Jaded, Disaffected Youth.

"Yeah. Honey! And other sweet stuff!" Christi bats her eyes at Josh. She has a crush on him and isn't shy about letting him know.

"They're, like, attracted to crap even more," Sherry says under her breath, so that Jill, sitting next to her, is the only one to hear. Jill offers a rare grin and high-fives her.

They continue watching YouTube. Jill pulls up a video of some awful screamo band that nobody else has heard of.

A few seconds into the so-called song, Josh leaps up from his seat, still waving his hands around his head.

"That's it!" he announces. "I can't take any more. I'm outta here."

"Is that fly still bugging you?" Christi looks disappointed. "Jill, you got any Raid?"

"I'm sure we do. Somewhere," Jill replies without looking away from the TV screen. "But I'm not spraying it down here. That stuff stinks."

"Aw, don't worry about it," Josh says, heading toward the stairs. "I need to get home, anyway. I wanna work out some. Gotta keep up with my weight training for football."

Christi gazes at him as he speaks, her dopey, worshipful expression getting even dopier and more worshipful at the mention of football.

"See ya," she calls as Josh heads upstairs, still waving an arm around his head.

"Yeah," he mutters, and leaves.

Jill mercifully switches to Netflix. Everybody's seen the first season of Abnormal Objects, but they agree to binge-watch it again because it's so awesome. They're on the fourth episode when the doorbell starts ringing, over and over.

"Who in the heck . . ." Jill mutes the TV. Everybody gets up from the white fake-leather sectional and heads for the staircase leading to the main floor. Jill reaches the staircase first. She puts her foot on the first step—and then they hear the sound of the front door being flung open.

Apparently, Josh didn't bother locking it on his way out.

The fight-or-flight reflex they learned about in biology class last year does not take effect: all of them freeze. Could this be a home invasion robbery? None have occurred here in Frogwood, but in Houston, less than two hours away, they happen all the time.

Sherry tells herself it's just Josh, returning after finally getting rid of the offending fly. Sherry's mind races, and one crazy thought after another flits through her mind. Perhaps Josh was able to crush the fly, in mid-flight, between his palms. The flies in this part of Texas are plentiful, and rabid. Fly-crushing between the palms is an acquired skill for many of the fine citizens of Frogwood. Such a skill requires excellent reflexes, and Josh certainly possesses these; his prowess on the football field proves it.

Her mind runs out of inane thoughts, and her heart pounds as she waits for what will come next. Adrenaline pumps through her veins and tingles as it fills her muscles, preparing her for a fight, if need be. Flight won't do much good. Here in the basement, there's nowhere to run, and there's no way out except for the stairs . . . which lead directly to the front door. Where whoever-it-is presumably waits for them.

A voice calls out, making her and the rest of them jump. "Is anyone here? I know you're here! Where are you?"

It's Mrs. Walker, Josh's mom. And she sounds rather unhappy.

The four teenagers let out relieved sighs. Sherry's knees start to buckle, but she resists the urge to sink to the carpet. She feels a stronger urge to pee but doesn't think her legs will make it to either bathroom; they're both on the main floor.

Tom, the smoother-talking of the smooth-talking Taylors, speaks up. "We're downstairs, Mrs. Walker," he says in a mock-respectful voice. "Josh left a few hours ago." You'd have to know him pretty well to pick up on the amused sarcasm in his tone.

Mrs. Walker stomps down the stairs so fast that Sherry's worried she might trip and start doing aerial cartwheels at any moment. When she reaches the basement, she puts her hands on her hips and glares at each teenager before speaking.

"How about putting on your masks while I'm here?" Mrs. Walker demands. The group scurries to comply.

"Why," she then continues with barely-contained fury, "did you give my son drugs?"

Nobody knows what to say. Tom turns away slightly and shields his face with one hand, trying to hide the fact that he's laughing.

None of the others see the humor in the situation.

Christi looks offended. "We didn't give him any drugs, Mrs. Walker," she says. "We don't use drugs."

This is basically true. The guys in the group are so into sports that they'd never jeopardize their eligibility. As for Christi, Jill, and Sherry: they once tried a joint that Jill had found in her older brother's sock drawer. It made her and Sherry laugh uncontrollably until they threw up. Christi broke out into hives and had to be taken to the emergency room, where she was given a shot and told that she had an allergy to cannabis. This effectively killed any curiosity they had in trying anything else.

"He was acting a little weird, though," Christi continues. "He was getting really bothered by this fly that wouldn't leave him alone. That's why he left."

"The fly," Mrs. Walker says. "Oh, yes, the fly. He thinks the damn thing followed him home! He thinks—he thinks—he thinks it was talking to him!"

Tom gives up on trying to hide his laughter.

Mrs. Walker whirls to face him and draws back her hand like she's going to slap him. Then she seems to change her mind and throws both hands into the air.

"You think it's funny, do you?" she snarls. Mrs. Walker notices that Sherry seems shocked that she is almost crying. "Do you think it's funny that my son was frightened enough to run all the way home? Do you think it's funny that the fly kept biting him in the neck until tripped and fell into a ditch? Do you think it's funny that my son now has a sprained ankle? And will likely be off the football team for the rest of the season?"

At the mention of "sprained ankle," Tom stops laughing as abruptly as if someone's hit his OFF switch.

Mrs. Walker takes a few deep breaths.

"I don't know why I bothered coming here," Mrs. Walker says. "And I don't know why Josh feels the need to hang around with a bunch of smart-aleck, drug-pushing losers like you!"

She storms back up the stairs. The entire house seems to shake as the front door slams.

They all stare at one another.

Christi is the only one who's able to speak.

"Weird," she observes. "Really. Freaking. Weird."

***

Sherry walks toward her group's cafeteria table. She's always the last of them to arrive for lunch; her Spanish II class, which meets before, is on the other side of the school.

Usually, the others are already seated by the time she gets here. Heck, they're usually half-finished with their lunches. But today, Jill's the only one present.

"Where is everybody?" Sherry asks as she sets her tray on the far end of table.

Jill shrugs. "Dunno. Josh wasn't in Chemistry. He might be taking a day or two off, though, with the sprained ankle. The Taylors weren't in history. I don't have any classes with Christi until after lunch. But I always pass her in the halls a few times." She stares thoughtfully at a Cutey-Fruity Bite and pops it into her ebony-lipsticked mouth, which shouldn't look right with her blue-tinted hair, yet somehow does. "I haven't seen her today, though."

"Wow." Sherry opens her own bag of Cutey-Fruity Bites and inhales three of them. "If Christi's absent, then this must be the Apocalypse." Christi isn't the best student, but her attendance record is stellar. She often brags that she hasn't missed a day since getting her appendix out during Kindergarten. One of the leading school fashionistas, Christi feels obligated to present her classmates with continual examples of smokin' hot style.

"Could it be that the psycho fly is harassing them, too?" Jill asks. She inspects her cellophane package for more Cutey-Fruity Bites. Finding none, she crumples the small, shiny package adorned with smiling fruits and settles for a French fry. "Could it be that we're next?"

Sherry stuffs her last Cutey-Fruity Bite back into the package. The rubbery, fluorescent-yellow, vaguely banana-shaped blob suddenly seems as repulsive as a dead slug.

"Don't say that. It's . . . well, that whole thing with Josh. It's just plain creepy. And now . . . with him and all of the others absent . . ."

Jill laughs and flips her hand dismissively. "Hey, don't worry. I was just joking. There's probably just a flu bug going around." She stuffs two French fries into her mouth, then shields the lower half of her face with her hand so she can talk without looking too gross. "This is Frogwood, Texas. A.K.A. Swampville, USA. There's always a flu bug going around."

***

Sherry is sleeping soundly. Correction: she's trying to sleep soundly. Something is making an absurd amount of noise. Something tiny yet amazingly annoying keeps brushing against her ear.

Her eyes flicker open for a split second. It's still pitch-black in her room, which means it's not yet time to wake up. She burrows her head into her pillow and almost manages to fall back asleep.

But the noise and the continual, annoying tickle against her ear resume.

In the morning, she'll tell herself that what happened next was only a dream. But she'll know, even as she tells herself this, that it really happened; and she'll also know that she will not admit this to herself, nor discuss the incident with anyone else.

Ever.

The buzzing grows more intense. She's entered that stage of half-sleep, half-wakefulness in which she's aware of what's going on around her but cannot move. She remembers reading something on an internet site about this. It's called "sleep paralysis."

The buzzing evolves into a kind of talking. A hybrid speech/buzz which is obscene, terrifying.

"My old man had it wrong," the speech/buzz shouts into her ear. "I didn't come back as a bird. I came back as a fly."

Sherry isn't surprised by this information: a part of her knew, as soon as Josh left Jill's basement, that this was what had happened.

"Flies live an average of twenty-eight days. You don't know what I'll be next time. For that matter, neither do I."

There's a brief interlude of staticky noise. Sherry decides this must be the sound of the fly laughing. She wonders if her biology teacher is aware of the fact that flies can laugh. And talk, even.

"I might come back as the copperhead that lives under your front porch," the fly informs her. "Or the neighbor's pit bull that always manages to jump the fence . . . or a baby who grows up to become a serial killer. A serial killer who moves into the house next door to you—and your husband—and your kids." The grotesque travesty of speech makes the threatening tone even more horrifying.

Yet Sherry can't even open her eyes—let alone scream, or run away.

If she could talk, she'd say: Dude! I didn't do anything! So why are you bugging me? No pun intended, of course!

Then she remembers what Jill said: he had a crazy-bad temper . . . ended up getting expelled . . .

The crazy-bad temper has apparently extended to the guy's current incarnation as a fly.

Awesome.

"You weren't making fun of my old man. You even stopped the others," the fly concedes, as though he's read her mind; and Sherry wonders: Is the darn thing telepathic, too?

"That's why I'm giving you and your one friend—the cute Emo chick—a hall pass this time. The others, though—they got more than the warning I'm giving you and Emo Chick. They got what was coming to them. They keep messing with my old man, and they'll get something even worse," he promises.

"And if you ever decide to join in—so help me—you will, too!"

EARL AND CHESTER

By Ed Wise

1. Chester the Jester

The letter made Chester smile. "Finally," he mumbled over the cacophony of voices in the high school hallway. He was about to put the letter into the neat locker when a hairy knuckled paw reached over his shoulder and snatched it away.

"Who in hell sent you something?" the voice asked.

Chester discretely removed his wide-framed black glasses, slid them in the locker, closed the door, and turned.

Earl, white tee under a black leather jacket, bright red hair and peach fuzz on his chin, grinned down, his gold tooth sparkling. Chester tried to retrieve the letter, but much like a puppet master, Earl repeatedly jerked it out of reach.

Earl squinted at the paper. "Who's John Hopkins?"

Chester grinned and shrugged.

Clay (Cleybert to his parents), short, thin, dressed the same as Earl, crept up and whispered in his boss's ear. "My brother said he'll get us a keg. He wants a hundred."

Earl held the letter high, then turned his head to Clay. "They cost fifty."

"I know. He said a hundred."

"Fuck." Earl passed the letter over his shoulder while he glared at Chester. "What's it say?"

Clay glanced at the letter as the crowd grew behind them.

"Dingle berry's going to medical school. Apparently, he got the highest MCAT score of anyone applying, 524. Full ride."

Earl's grip on Chester tightened. "Listen ass hole. Bella said you were starring at her tits when you were cuttin' up them frogs Monday."

Chester struggled to turn to Chester. "She asked me to help her while Mrs. Harper was in the bathroom."

"If you don't know the difference between tits and frog guts maybe you should be workin' at the garage with your old man instead of going to a fancy ass college."

"Sorry," Chester squeaked.

Clay passed the letter back to Earl.

Earl put the letter against the locker, spun Chester around, then pushed his face into it. "Congratulations, geek. A rich doctor can afford to pay me the hundred bucks he owes me." Earl ground Chester's face into the letter with one hand, extracted Chester's wallet with the other, then passed it over his shoulder. "How much's he got?"

Clay peered in. "Forty." The empty wallet dropped to the floor.

Hot, wet breath and spittle blew into Chester's ear. "You owe me sixty bucks," growled Earl. The letter was crunched up and dropped next to the wallet. "Bring it to the float party tonight or you'll be in a cooler tomorrow." Chester's face was pulled back by his hair, then bounced off the locker. Earl turned and the sea of on lookers parted as he sauntered down the hallway with Clay in tow.

Chester was left to retrieve his treasure. He flattened the letter, put it back in its envelope. Feeling liquid run to his mouth, he stuck his tongue out to the familiar metallic taste. "Damn."

He opened the locker and peered into the mirror on the doors back side. He saw a rather handsome, but geekish, dark haired, near man, with a small trail of blood running from his nose. He wiped the blood, a tear, then slammed the door shut. "We'll see who's laughing in a few years, douche bag," he mumbled.

Chester made his way to the end of the hallway and found a folding table staffed by two students. A professional banner read,

"Vote for Your King and Queen". Underneath someone had hand written, "and Jester."

Chester picked a ballot up. On it, there were three boxes and a name on each, Earl Mamba, King, Bella Turdle, Queen, Chester Ridgefield, Court Jester.

"What the?" Chester exclaimed as he looked at the two students.

The one with the bandaged nose remained silent, while Black Eye replied, "Sorry."

2. Major Ridgefield?

The three-two ranch was spartan but tidy. Blondie, an aging golden retriever, dozed by Chester's feet at the book-covered dining room table.

Mark Ridgefield, crew cut, muscular, in oil stained coveralls came in the rear door.

"Hey," Chester said as he looked up from a book and smiled.

"You gonna be done in time to go to the alley with me tonight? We lock a spot in the tournament with a win. I could use the luck."

"Sure Dad."

"I'm gonna grab a shower." His father picked up an AP Biology book. "Your mother would have been proud. You've busted your hump and it's time for the payoff." He smiled at Chester and muffed his hair. "Any word from any of your schools?"

Chester slid the letter from Johns Hopkins under a book. "Soon, I hope."

"The corps could use someone like you. As a surgeon, you'd start as a major. Sweet pay, make friends for life."

"I know. I'm thinkin' about it."

"Don't underestimate the value of having people you can count on. I'm not gonna be around forever."

Chester went back to his book. "Thinkin' about it, Dad."

"Just sayin.' Look at Charley and me. Been together since Nam, twenty years now."

Chester, head down in his book. "Got it."

Mark took a step towards the hallway.

Chester looked back up. "I need sixty bucks for an application."

Mark turned. "I thought you were done with those?" He pulled out a worn wallet, removed the cash and gave Chester forty-two. "I'll have to get the rest from the bank."

"No problem. I want to send it in Monday morning."

Mark took a step.

"I also need to borrow the car for a few minutes." Mark turned to Chester. "They want someone to pick up supplies for the homecoming float."

"Sure. Be back at six-thirty." Mark tossed Chester the keys.

3. Chester's First Beer

Chester snatched the keys and trotted out the rear door. He removed a sheet from the driver's seat of the ten-year-old sedan, folded it, and set it on the rear floorboard next to a yellow pencil.

Chester drove to the float barn and parked next to a bevy of dilapidated cars. He hesitantly approached the open door. *Stairway to Heaven* blended with the chatter of a party in the background. He poked his head in and was amazed at the scene before him. Of the thirtyish students inside, half worked on a nearly complete parade float; the rest, save two, rushed about with supplies. Chester cautiously made his way to the keg where Earl sat on a throne made of hay bales. Clay dispensed beer.

Snickering and mumbling followed Chester as he made his way to Earl, each step seeming like a mile. He silently handed the King forty-two dollars. "I'll have to give you the rest Monday."

"All right douche bag. But it's twenty-five then." Chester met Earl's gaze, his gold tooth glinting. "Interest sucks, don't it?"

Chester turned and took a step.

"Where-da-ya think you're going?" Earl asked.

Chester turned. "I had to borrow Dad's car. He needs it for bowling."

"Well he's gonna be late. You're a member of court. You have civic duties, moron. You're going to work on the float while I make sure this keg gets drained properly." Earl nodded at Clay, who passed Chester a beer. "And you'll match me beer for beer."

* *   *

Chester stumbled into the bathroom and peed. He flipped the mirror back on the medicine cabinet and rummaged for aspirin. He washed three down, closed the mirror, and was sickened further at the sight. "Ugh." His skin was pale, eyes bloodshot, with bags under them.

He made his way downstairs and found his father reading a newspaper.

Mark set the paper down next to a steaming cup of coffee and a box of top shelf condoms. "Have fun last night?" He asked.

Chester sat on the sofa and shrugged his shoulders.

"You don't know?"

"Don't remember," Chester mumbled, as he lowered his head.

"You disappointed me. I had to have Charley pick me up; then I had to have him come and get you when they called." Mark shook his head. "We had to forfeit the match and dropped two spots in the standings. You're grounded for a month."

Chester met his father's eye, a tear welling in his own. "Sorry." He looked down.

"I'm not going to lecture you about being responsible with your commitments and excessive drinking. Hopefully that pounding in your head's enough." Mark sipped his coffee. "Who's the girl?"

Chester stared at his father. "What?"

"The girl?"

"I don't know what you're talking about. I remember going into the barn and drinking a beer; then it's blank until I woke up next to the toilet."

Mark shook his head. "Casual sex leads to serious problems." He handed Chester the condoms. "Even though your mother wouldn't have wanted me to, I'm not going to lecture to you more about premarital sex, either. We did it ourselves. Just use a quality condom next time." Mark sipped his coffee. "And clean up after yourself. That car and this house are all we have. The sheet's to keep it clean. You might have used it."

Mark went back to the paper. "I put some cleaning supplies next to the sink. I suggest you use the gloves."

Chester gathered the supplies and trudged to the car. On the back seat he found a plain white condom wrapper. He discovered the used device itself on the sheet, which still laid neatly folded on the floorboard. He held back some vomit, picked the condom up with the pencil, and held it to eye level.

It was broken and dripped. "Fuck."

4. I'm Late

Voluptuous, dark-haired Bella answered the doorbell in a pretty Christmas sweater.

Earl pushed into the house, grabbed her hand, and led her to the stairway. "How long will they be gone?" He asked.

Bella pulled him to the sofa, sat, and patted the spot next to her.

"Sit," she said as she pointed at the sofa.

Earl obeyed, then reached for her breast.

She gently pushed his hand away. "No. Wait." She looked him in the eye. "I'm late."

"I forgive you." Earl went in for a kiss, his hand extending towards the breast again.

With a little more force, she pushed him away. "No . . . I'm pregnant. We have to get married."

"What? We're not getting married. We can't. I joined the navy." The usual sparkle on Earl's gold tooth dimmed.

Bella, amazed, shook her head. "What the hell, Earl?"

"I'm going to see the world." Earl rolled up his sleeve. He pulled back the corner of a large bandage to reveal a gaudy anchor with some illegible scrawl underneath it. "Check it out, I even got a tattoo."

"You said you were going to community college with me. We were going to graduate, get jobs, start a family."

Earl slid closer, reached down and gently stroked her knee. "Change of plans. I didn't get accepted."

Stern faced, Bella stared at Earl. "Everyone gets accepted."

"Apparently not." Earl's hand advanced and was rebuffed once again. He frowned. "I had to go to plan 'B.'"

Bella shook her head. "You were going to tell me when?"

"After the holidays." Earl's tooth glinted as he scooched closer.

Bella shook her head again. "Damn it, Earl."

Earl's hand moved up to her knee. "I don't see a problem. Just get rid of it."

She roughly picked up Earl's hand and dropped it on his crotch. "It's my baby. I'm not getting rid of it. Besides, you know how Daddy is. He'd disown me if I have a baby and ain't married."

"He's not that bad. He'll forgive you." Earl's hand slid back.

"He's a deacon for Christ's sake." She looked him in the eye. "What are we gonna do?"

"What are YOU gonna do. I'm on plan B. You might get one of those yourself." Earl's hand slowly crept towards her.

"This is serious. If you're going to be gone, I'm going to need a job. A good job. I need my LPN cert." She shook her head. "And someone to take care of me. Can you at least send money?" Like a mongoose, she watched his hand slowly rise, her own poised to pounce on it once more. It passed her thigh, then her breast, to her neck, where it landed.

He turned her head towards him, his eyes glinting once more. "They don't pay much, and I'll need most of what they give me for port calls. I'll send what I can."

Bella bowed down in tears. "There's no choice. We have to get married."

"No, not exactly." Earl slid over, cradled her head on his shoulder and hugged her. "Look I have an idea. You can go to college, get your LGN."

"LPN," Bella said.

"Whatever," Earl said as he shook his head. "You'll even have someone help you with the baby. I signed up for four years. After I'm done, I'll come home. Then I can take care of the kid while you work. What-da-ya think?"

Bella glanced up and wiped a tear. "Really? That's your plan? I'm pregnant. I need to be married."

Earl picked up her hand and led her to the stairway. "I said I have idea. I'll tell you upstairs after we're done." Earl reached into his pocket, pulled out a condom in a plain white wrapper, and held it up to her.

5. Chester the Molester

Chester stopped in his tracks when he rounded the corner of the house and saw two cars in the driveway. His father's and a police cruiser. He cautiously walked towards the kitchen door and noticed "Chief" stenciled on the cruiser.

He crept into the house and found his father and Chief Turdle staring at him from the dining room. He set his books on the table and looked questioningly at his father.

"We have a problem we need to talk about. Come on into the living room."

Chester was led into the room and found a conservatively dressed, middle aged woman holding a weeping Bella.

Chief Turdle glared at Bella, then Chester. "Is he the one?"

Bella glanced at Chester and nodded. "I told him I didn't want to go all the way. He wouldn't stop," she sobbed.

Chester's jaw dropped.

His father shook his head, moved to hold Chester, and whispered in his ear. "We'll get through this. Be tough."

"That's rape, son," the chief said. "She's pregnant. You're either getting married or going to jail. Take your pick."

"I'm going to Hopkins in the fall."

"You were accepted?" his father exclaimed with an ear to ear smile.

Chester nodded.

"Not unless they have classes in prison. You should have thought about that before you molested my daughter." Chief Turdle pulled his hand cuffs from his belt, held them up, then nodded at Bella. "Which one's it gonna be?"

6. Martin's

Chester pushed a broom in the mom and pop drug store. A well-dressed woman in her sixties, wearing a feathered purple fedora and carrying a tiny dog in a hand, bag waved at him.

"Excuse me, Chester," she said.

Chester set the broom in a corner and wiped his hands on his apron, then walked to her.

"Good afternoon Mrs. Pompadour," Chester said as he reached his hand out to the dog. "How's Musky today?" Musky licked Chester's hand; Chester scratched his ears in return.

"Just fine. You're a sweetheart for asking." She pointed at the shelf of laxatives. "Which of these is best?"

Chester pulled one out and handed it to her. "This one, I think. But you should ask Mr. Martin. I'm not allowed to give medical advice." Chester pointed to the counter in the rear. A spectacled elderly man was busy filling a prescription behind the counter. "Why don't you take it, and ask him if it's best."

Pompadour pinched his cheek. "Thanks Chester. I'm so glad you're here to help."

She took the laxative to the rear counter and left Chester to resume sweeping.

Late that evening, Chester put his apron away and picked out a large package of diapers. He turned to Mr. Martin who was filling another prescription.

"I'm headed out. I've got a pack of diapers; can you take it off my pay?"

"No worries Chester. My treat. I appreciate your hard work."

Chester walked to the bus stop on the corner. His eye was drawn to the bank across the street. Workers were installing a bulky machine in the front wall. Chester's eyebrows lowered and he scrunched his chin. "Hmm." A bus drove up and blocked his view. He got on.

"Hey Chester," said the driver.

"Hey," Chester replied as he mindlessly sat behind the driver. "What's with the bank?"

The driver turned slightly towards Chester, but kept his eye on the road. "New ATM," he mumbled as he nodded and smiled. "You can get money any time you want. If you have any, that is."

7. Oops, It Happened Again

Earl rolled off his sofa and slapped his feet on a pizza box. It crunched as he stood. He stumbled onward and stubbed his toe on an empty liquor bottle. "Damn." Finally, he reached the kitchen of the fifty-year-old trailer. Opening the refrigerator, he found a pile of condiment packets in a drawer, a bulging storage container with lasagna covered in blue cheese, a quart of milk on its side in a puddle, and an empty cardboard container of cheap beer.

"Shit," he exclaimed as he slammed the door shut.

Earl continued trudging through debris. He stopped in the bathroom for a piss before reaching the bedroom. On the nightstand was an open beer, a clock that read 2:45 p.m., and two large pictures turned down. He walked to the bed, moved a pillow in a crater, sat on a white condom wrapper, picked up the phone, and pushed the buttons for the only number he knew.

"Third floor east," a woman said from St. Gabriel's Extended Care.

"Bella Ridgefield." Earl picked up the beer, sniffed it, then took a pull. He grimaced, spit a greenish glob onto the vinyl floor, then took another pull.

"Bella," echoed from the phone.

Earl slid back onto the bed, his ass contoured itself perfectly in the crater. "Hey Baby."

Bella looked around the nurse's station. "I told you not to call me at work."

"Sorry, I've got a medical condition." Earl glanced at the bulge in his boxers and grinned.

Bella shook her head. "Let me guess. You've a growth in your pants."

"Yup, and it needs attention. Can you stop by after work?" Earl took another sip.

Bella grinned and looked towards the ceiling. "Lucy's sick."

"Can't nimrod watch her? It'll only take a minute."

"He's got work, and Martin's getting tired of him being late."

"You said the old man loved him; he'll deal with it. Have him work a few hours off the clock again." Earl took another pull, crunched the can, and tossed it in a corner. "Did she like the block's I sent for her birthday?"

Bella smiled and twirled the cord around her finger. "Yes, but she's only two. And a girl. Get the big one's next time."

"Sure thing, baby. I'll see you in an hour."

"Ok. But listen Earl. We need to talk. Please be sober."

"Will do baby. Love ya."

"Love you, too."

"Oh, and Bella, pick up a twelve pack on your way." Earl hung up and glinted.

He stood the pictures on the nightstand up. One was a picture of Bella in a nurse's outfit, receiving a diploma at a graduation ceremony. The other a red headed two-year-old. Earl laid back on the bed for a quick nap.

8. Night School

Chester sat, with an apron on, reading a brochure at the dining table of his father's home. The cover read, "Adam's County Community College." It showed a picture of a happy woman in a nurse's uniform, and below that, "You Can Get an RN at our Night School in Just a Few Years.".

In the corner of the room was playpen with a two-year-old. She slept, clutching a stuffed Big Bird and sucking her thumb.

There was a knock on the kitchen door. Chester glanced at a clock that read 3:15 p.m., put the brochure down, and answered it.

"Chief Turdle, come on in."

The Chief slowly entered and removed his hat. Chester wiped his hand on the apron and offered it to Turdle.

"You're about ten minutes late." Chester nodded towards the sleeping toddler. "I just got her down."

The chief nodded. "Chester, you'd better sit." He guided Chester into a chair and sat opposite him.

"Who?" Chester said as he stared at the chief.

"Bella's fine. I'm afraid it's your dad. There was an accident at the garage. Apparently, he forgot to put a stand under a truck he was working on and the jack failed. There was nothing they could do."

Chester's head collapsed into his hands.

"You want a drink?" Turdle asked.

Chester shook his head.

"You want me to stay with you, or be alone for a while?"

"Alone."

The chief patted him on the back, then picked up the baby. "I'm gonna to take Lucy to our house for the afternoon. The Mrs. will bring something by later."

The chief left as Chester sobbed.

9.   One of Those Tests

Bella walked into the trailer's bedroom. She smiled at the pictures of her and Lucy, then glanced at Earl's clock. It read 3.32 p.m. She sat in a ratty old chair and stared at Earl. He snored peacefully in bed. She tossed a not quite empty beer can at his head that connected. Stale beer splashed on Earl's face.

"Hey," Earl said as he wiped his face with his pillow. He sat up and rubbed his head. "Did you get the beer?"

"Fridge."

"Get me one, wouldja?"

"In a minute." She sat further up in the chair. "Listen Earl, I took one of those tests. I'm pregnant again."

Earl stretched and wiped sleep from his eyes. "Why tell me?"

"You know why."

"So, what's the problem?" Earl got up and reached for Bella's breast.

She pushed his hand away. "We barely have enough to get by on now. All the cards are maxed. He'd throw a fit if he knew I was paying your rent and stuff."

Earl walked out of the bedroom. "Have him get another job."

"Martin's working him sixty a week. He watches Lucy while I'm at work. He's got to sleep sometime." Bella got up and followed.

"Pussy." Earl walked to the refrigerator, grabbed a beer, and went into the living area.

"Have you had any luck finding a job?" Bella asked.

"It's tough out there." Earl sat at on one end of the sofa and opened the beer. "What about his dad?"

"He's working like a dog, too." Bella cleared a spot on the other end of the sofa and sat. "He fell asleep during dinner last night."

"Another pussy. No surprise." Earl finished his beer, crushed the can, and tossed it in a corner. "Grab me a refill wouldja?"

Bella got up and got a beer from the fridge. "Look, Earl. I don't want to do this anymore. You said we'd be together after you got out of the navy."

"I thought it was going to be four years. How could I know they were going to boot my ass?" Earl took a pull from the beer. "What about your parents?"

"They found out about you. They said they'd take Lucy, but they're not going to give me anything until I leave you."

"Well that's not gonna happen." Earl slid closer to Bella. "Doesn't he have life insurance? Have him cash it in, or better we could arrange for an accident."

"Martin got him a policy, ten grand."

"That wouldn't last us very long." Earl's free hand slid up her leg.

She grabbed it and met Earl's eye. "You're not thinking of killing him, are you? He's great with Lucy."

"Not me. I'm too smart for that. If you want something done, get someone else to do it for you." He glinted at her.

She pushed his hand away. "I'm not going to do it!"

Earl moved his hand back and started stroking her inner thigh. "Of course, not you, baby." Earl's hand moved up her leg. "Hmm. I heard some idiot fell in front of a subway in New York. His family got two million from the city. Shoulda been a rail or something."

"We don't have a subway, Earl!"

"No, but we have buses." Earl stood in front of her and unzipped his pants. "I'll tell you what I have in mind while you take care of me."

*   *   *

Earl zipped his pants and sat.

"I don't know Earl," Bella said as she wiped her lip.

"It's the only way. There should be a bunch of condom wrappers in the bedroom. Just spread a few around the house. Places he'll find them. Not too obvious. Let me know when he asks about them."

10. Earl's Plan

Chester was pushing his broom in Martin's when Earl strolled in.

"How's it going, Chester?" Earl smiled at Chester, his tooth glinting. "I haven't seen you since you stole my girl. I'd ask how she's doing? But I already know," Earl said, then winked at Chester.

Chester stopped and glared at Earl with his broom tightly gripped in front of himself. "Is there something I can help you with, Earl?"

"Yeah, I need condom's."

Chester led Earl to the display counter near the rear. He pointed to the top shelf. "I think those are best. But you should ask Mr. Martin."

Earl smiled again. "No, Bella likes those down there." Earl pointed at the white box. "Hand me a pack."

Chester picked up the box and slowly passed it to him. Earl accepted the box, but Chester didn't release it.

"Are you sleeping with my wife?" Chester asked.

"I wouldn't call it sleep Chester, but if you mean, am I having sex with her, yes. I've been pounding her at least three times a week. How about you? Is she giving you any?" Earl glinted again. "Haven't you wondered how she got pregnant this time? Why Lucy has red hair?"

The broom fell from Chester's grip. His hands balled into fists, and his knuckles whitened.

Earl pointed at a security camera which was aimed at them. "I wouldn't if I were you. Pretty boys don't last long in jail." Earl smiled at Chester. "You're a fucking loser. Why don't you go home and ask her? You know where the bus stop is."

Chester scrunched up his apron, tossed it on a shelf, then stormed out.

Chester stood on the corner waiting for the light to change. In front of him was a freshly broken curb. There was something odd about it and his eyes were drawn to it.

"Well, well, I haven't seen you in years," came a familiar voice from behind.

Chester spun around and his eyes bulged. "Clay! What're you doing here?"

"Same as you, waiting for the bus."

A bus roared. Chester turned to the street and shook his head. The bus sped towards a green light. With two hands, Clay pushed Chester's shoulders.

Chester's eyes bulged; his arms spun as he tried to regain his balance. Then he fell into the street where #14 finally ended his pain.

11. Another Homecoming

Chester had been gone nearly four years. Even so, he didn't really want to come home; he was comfortable. Nice and warm, comfy and cozy. Except he wanted more. More than to just hear Camilla's voice. He wanted to see her, hold her, and help her.

Camilla needed him, and he had a lot of experience with her problems. It turned out that Sofia was a cheating whore. Marco wasn't the father of her child; it was Jose's, or possibly Juan's. That morning at 10:10, Chester heard Camilla cursing Valeria for dropping out of college to pursue a career as an actress.

"Can you believe it?" Camilla asked as she watched the TV from a recliner next to Chester's hospital bed.

"*Muy estupido,*" he said. Chester did a double take and pondered how he'd come to learn Spanish.

Camilla's jaw dropped and she slowly turned from "*Momentos de Nuestras Vidas*" (Moments of Our Lives) to her patient. "*Santo cielo,*" (holy crap) she exclaimed as she saw Chester's eyes open for the first time.

"Don't worry, I'll talk to Valeria," Chester said.

Camila turned the TV off and sped out of the room.

Dr. Goodhert, fifties, white hair, white lab coat, soon rushed in and checked Chester's vitals. "Well I'll be damned. You've been in perfect health for years. I was wondering if I'd missed something." He smiled at Chester. "How are you feeling?"

"Where am I?" Chester asked as he peered around.

Goodhert waved a pen light in Chester's eyes. "St. Mary's Long-Term Convalescence Center." Goodhert poked and prodded Chester. "Remarkable. What's the last thing you remember?"

"Seeing a bus rush towards my face."

"Well, a lot has happened; let me fill you in."

"I think I need a drink," Chester said as he rubbed sleep from his eyes.

"Are you sure you're ready?" Goodhert asked as he continued to poke and prod Chester.

Chester smiled at Camilla and nodded.

Goodhert turned to Camilla. "There's a bottle in my bottom drawer, get it for us, would you?"

"Left side?" Camilla asked as she left.

"No. This is a special day. Get me the good one." Goodhert turned back to Chester and smiled. "Better bring a bucket of ice and three glasses, too. This is gonna take a while."

Chester stared at Goodhert. "My slut wife?"

"Prison. She, Earl, and Clay were convicted of attempted murder, among other things."

Chester looked questioningly at Goodhert.

"She tried to sue the city. Their insurance company retrieved the video from the ATM across the street. It showed Clay pushing you." Goodhert stopped and stared into Chester's eyes. "Marvelous thing, advanced technology."

Camilla returned and fixed three drinks.

"They have cameras?" Chester inquired.

"Yup, seems like they're everywhere these days."

"What shall we toast to?" Camilla asked as she moved to Chester's side and handed him a drink.

Chester smiled at her. Their hands touched as he accepted the drink. "What else? ATMs."

They sipped their drinks. "To ATMs."

Chester's free hand moved to Camilla's and he held it gently. She withdrew it, glanced at Goodhert who was preoccupied with Chester, then slid it back and smiled.

Goodhert sat next to Chester and sipped his drink. "It was like rats fighting for the last scrap of wood from a sinking ship after Clay was brought in. They couldn't line up fast enough to turn on each other."

"Lucy?" Chester asked.

"Adopted by the Turdles."

Chester turned to his nightstand. On it was the framed crinkled letter from Johns Hopkins.

Goodhert sat back and looked at Chester. "You're still a young man. Any ideas what you want to do with your life?"

Chester smiled at the letter, then turned to Camilla. "A coupla things come to mind."

CONTACT US

Connect with us at:

CovingtonWritersGroup@outlook.com

and

www.facebook.com@Covingtonwritersgroup

www.ingramcontent.com/pod-product-compliance
Lightning Source LLC
Chambersburg PA
CBHW051929240626
47153CB00004B/1424